Jolly Olde
Teenage ALIEN

by

Jane Greenhill

Jolly Olde Teenage ALIEN

Cover Art by *Jennifer Greeff*

The Wild Rose Press, Inc.
PO Box 708
Adams Basin, NY 14410-0708
Visit us at www.thewildrosepress.com

Publishing History
First Edition, 2021
Trade Paperback ISBN 978-1-5092-3675-6
Digital ISBN 978-1-5092-3676-3

Published in the United States of America

"Whoa," Jocko said. "Calm down. You're off on a rant and besides, we don't need to resort to name-calling. We're all adults here." He took a sip of tea and flipped open the newspaper. "Keep good karma flowing."

I'll good karma him in a minute. I stomped out through the hallway, took a look in the mirror, and was proud of what I saw. I tucked my hair behind my ears, shoved my shoulders back, grabbed my suitcase and with my *hanaglug* slung over my back, I opened and slammed the door shut when I heard the sound of breaking glass.

The landing where I stood swayed a fraction of a millimeter and I grabbed the wall, so I didn't topple over. My stomach felt a tad queasy, and I swallowed, before pushing myself off from the wall and taking a deep breath.

Cautiously I opened the door and saw the black-and-white tiled floor covered with broken glass.

"Oh, Jocko, come and see what happened. I believe the one who owns the mirror is the one who gets the seven years bad luck." Freaky Freddie whispered.

"Never tick off a *femawl*," I calmly said, gently closing the door.

Dedication

To Geoff, Adam and Liam who fill my days with
laughter.
Yona who completes our family and Mrs.
Patriquin.

Chapter 1

"Wow, sis, I really know how to suck up," Ralb said, settling deeper into the maroon plush leather seats. More comfortable than anything I've ever sat on and to think I was on a private jet was too random to even contemplate. Music filled the air, a loop of Peach Acid's music played continuously.

Sure beat the method of transportation on my home planet of Zorca-twenty-three. There we had to travel by dragonfly or asteroid. Major uncomfortable!

"I'm not speaking to you." I ground out the words between clenched teeth.

"Why? What did I do?" He shrugged. "It wasn't my fault he ditched you."

"Shut up!" Anything to do with Josh was a real sore point with me. He was my first Earth mawlfriend, and I thought we were really going to be together forever. He'd even given me his ring. When you space travel with someone, especially someone from a completely different planet than yours, it tends to create somewhat of a bond, but he was AWOL. After we parted company in New Zealand, I thought we'd meet for dinner, but I haven't seen him since.

I didn't want to even flirt with the idea he was deceased. I'd done too much to keep him alive after the first time Suzz killed him. Yep, you read right. She killed my mawlfriend, stepped on him when we were in bug form. I guess that shows you how forgiving I am, that I didn't kill her myself, but actually she's somewhat of a friend. I mean, we did save the penguins together. But I couldn't think of any other reason, he wouldn't be here with me now, unless he couldn't be. He *jobed* me, he told me so.

"Right," I whispered to Ralb, not wanting the entire plane to hear our business. "It had absolutely nothing to do with Suzz."

"Not at all." He punched my arm, weakly I might add. "Besides, in case you haven't noticed, we're on our way to England, hello—home of Rockhedge Circle."

"Big whoop, a circle of ancient rocks." I was still furious with him. When I think of all I've done for him in my Earth lifetime, I left my home planet of Zorca-twenty-three, ventured via asteroid, not the easiest method of travel, let me tell you, to rescue him from the clutches of Suzz and what thanks do I get.

Nada none!

"That circle of rocks is going to get us back home," he reminded me.

"Yeah, well, knowing your history and all, I'm not putting any money on that one at the bookies." Twice now he's tried to get us home. First, we ended up in France and I got to meet Jason Montana, so okay that was kind of cool. Then the second time, he got us up on Suzz's SpaceMoonOne spaceship which was actually supposed to be just a movie set and we ended up in New Zealand. So, pardon me if I'm a little *scheckiple* that this time it's going to work.

"I tried my best," he smirked. "Maybe you'd like to be responsible for getting us all back home. If you think it's so easy, be my guest."

"Really! Well, I certainly couldn't do any worse. Consider it done. Pack your bags, my annoying bro, we're going home."

I turned my brain off. After all, I had to save my energy for space travel and nodded to my brother's seatmate. "Why don't you chat up Hildy there? It'll help pass the time."

The words were met by a scowl, not from my brother mind you, but from the humanoid—and I use the term loosely—beside him. With jet black hair plastered to her head, a style which wouldn't change in a monsoon, neck tattoos of snakes and, from what I could see, a vicious unicorn with fangs dripping blood. Her make-up—black paint dripping under her eyes and bright red lips—reminded me of a vampire movie.

So, to summarize, I'd hate to meet her in a dark alley and if I did, I'd be saying many prayers if I couldn't outrun her. I was glad I wasn't sitting beside her because I tend to talk a lot, (like you couldn't tell) and I didn't want to get on her wrong side. Or any of her sides, for that matter.

Peeling my eyes away from the train wreck of Ralb trying to win over the Queen of Darkness, no really that was her stage name. She was a member of the mega-hit band, Peach Acid and this was their plane. Not just any plane mind you, this was a reworked 747. I guess they could afford it thanks to the fact they'd recently had a number one hit with our own Suzzy Newsworthy.

Jocko and Freaky Freddie met Suzz, aka Suzzy Newsworthy, at a fundraising benefit for the Duck-Billed Platypus in Australia. Who knew the funny looking animal was on the verge of becoming extinct?

When I first knew her, she was plain old Suzz from Bedrocktown, then she became a singing sensation, and the powers that be, or more likely the publicity department, thought Suzzy Newsworthy sounded cooler. (Just to clarify, she's one and the same.) Ralb and I tagged along for the holiday. Frankly, after saving the world I needed the rest. Anyway, long story shorter, Ralb elbowed his way into an after-party where there was a life-sized platypus made of chocolate, and you guessed it.

I'm surprised you got it in one. You must have already met my brother. So, after he got in trouble for eating the display before the official photo shoot, Freaky Freddie came over and shook his chocolate covered hand.

"Hey, mate, that was totally awesome." Being the hound dog he was, Freaky Freddie eyed up Suzzy first, then me, then roved his eyes back to Suzzy.

"Hey, aren't you the chick who flew up in space for TZZ?" he asked, stepping into Suzzy's space.

Personally, I can't stand it when someone does that. I mean, keep your distance, and honor each person's individual area, but she didn't seem to mind.

"Well, yes, I am." She began to describe the highlights of our travel to the upper atmosphere. I didn't think we had too many. If it wasn't for Ralb's lack of navigational skills and a spilt cup of tea, which mucked up the controls, we went up, we came back down, landed in New Zealand, and saved the penguins. That pretty much summarized our adventure. But she managed to embellish it and make it seem like she was the best thing to hit space since your Space Port.

Well, after several publicity photos and dinners

which made the pages of The National Tabloid, it was only natural they joined forces and cut a deal with a record.

The rest, as they say, is history.

She sang the lead vocals for the Billboard hit, "Can't Take It With You." The song rushed past KPerryK's latest song and blew up the charts, remaining at number one for an unheard of twenty-five weeks. Everyone from the street cleaners to the President of the United States was caught humming the catchy phrase:

"Spend it now,
'cause you can't take it with you.
Buy the Farm and Rent the Cow,
'cause you can't take it with you.
Push the Daisies from underground
'cause you can't take it with you."

Even now, I can't get the tune out of my head—annoying like a toothache. Even when you hear the end of the song, it keeps on going on and on and on and on.

"Could you tell me where the bathroom is?" I asked the flight attendant who kept leaning over Jocko like she was his mother and he needed help tying his shoes.

"Sure, sweetie, just through that curtain and first door on your left. Don't open the door on your right or you might be walking on a cloud." She turned and spoke in my direction, but all her attention went towards Jocko.

"If you'd move a tad, I could get by," I said, sweetly. You never want to tick off anyone who could make your flight a living nightmare.

Plush carpet creamed through my toes as I walked

up the aisle towards the front of the plane. The 'occupied' light flashed on, so I read the emergency card outside the door. I think I could adhere to everything on it since I didn't smoke and had no intention of jumping out into the great beyond.

The sign switched to "unoccupied" and Hildy stepped out.

"It's all yours." I hadn't even noticed she had left my brother's side. She rubbed her hand along my arm as if to warm me up. "I hope we get to know each other quite a bit better than we already do."

"Sure," I said, unsure about what she meant. Anxious to get away, I stepped into the bathroom and quickly locked the door behind me.

It was quite unlike any airplane bathroom I'd ever seen. I'm not saying I'm an expert or anything, but the airplane movies I'd watched on my *wad* on my home planet of Zorca-twenty-three were nothing like this one. They were mostly metal and compact and didn't leave room for much else to do but your business. But this one was as far from the commercial flight washroom as I was to Chelsea Sims, who by the way was absolutely stunning on her wedding day.

For one thing, the toilet wasn't metal but rather a sweet shade of peach porcelain. The sink and mirror were on the opposite side, with a window on either side of the mirror. There was a hand dryer and towels fluffier than any sheep I'd ever seen. A four-walled glass shower was tucked in the corner and a bathtub for at least three people fitted along the back wall.

I have to say, I was impressed. I walked over to the toilet, almost out of breath from the distance I had to cross, and put the seat down before I could use it. I quickly did my business and washed and dried my hands on one of the towels.

Beside the sink was a basket filled with soaps, hand creams, shampoos, conditioners, toothbrushes, dental floss, and square foil packages which I had no clue what they were, but they were there if I did ever need them.

Reluctantly I left the room and headed back to my seat, avoiding all eye contact with Hildy.

Freaky Freddie chuckled as he wiped his hair off his forehead only to have it fall into place where it had been. "Hey, check out Jocko and his superstitions. He has to do the same things, in the same order, on every flight and before a concert." He counted off on his fingers. "One, he kisses his necklace."

I looked at the pendant on the chain and shivered. Why anyone would want to kiss, never mind wear, such a hideous piece of jewelry is way beyond me? I mean, who wants to have anything to do with a genuine horse shoe, the weight must have been crazy heavy?

"Two, he has to twirl the skull ring on his left index finger, not his right one mind you, but his left one, three times clockwise and six times counterclockwise."

Obviously, he heard Freaky Freddie's comments because he inserted his middle finger into the air, which I know from my Earth travels is not a welcoming gesture.

Situated between the window and Freaky Freddie, the drummer, I searched frantically for my seat belt, I really don't know what good it would do if we did take a header towards earth anytime soon. I mean, okay, it might stop me from flying around like there was zero gravity, and I guess that was the entire point. Let's face it. I was sure traveling in the lap of luxury, unlike five months ago.

I involuntarily shuddered as if someone walked across my grave site as I remembered the details of that flight. To summarize a tad for you, in case you missed the Persone Magazine article where I saved your planet, again, I'll give you the long story shorter version which wasn't in the article, the nitty-gritty behind the scenes of what really happened.

I'm a Teenage ALIEN.

My Zorca-twenty-three name is OAS, which Ralb likes to say stands for Older Annoying Sister, which we all know isn't the case. I'm actually quite helpful to him. I try to mentor him, try to let him look up to me by leading by example at least that's what I let my Parental Beings think. My earth name is APRIL—the letters represent Alien Person Representing Intelligent Life. I didn't know when I was given it, it stood for one of your spring months and my birthing wasn't even in April, but in June, which is totally confusing and almost like one of those April Fools jokes your planet loves so much to play on each other.

I feel I can tell you things and you look like the type of humanoid who could keep a secret. Anyway, hopefully I'm a good *judgement* of character. I traveled to Earth via an asteroid to save my stupid brother Ralb from Suzz, but I'm getting ahead of myself, and if I do that you'll get royally confused.

So, when I landed, or rather when we landed—Rotsen, my dandelion and I—we ended up in Bedrocktown. The town's citizens were getting sick, and Nicola my Earth BFF almost died. Well, insert cough here, I realized the town was being poisoned by E.coli. I told the town's doctor who gave everyone medicine and, well, no one died on my watch.

Fast forward to Ralb, Rotsen, Lehcarr (my Venus Fly Trap BFF), and I trying to get back to Zorca-twenty-three, the planet where we originated. Ralb didn't read the instructions (enough said there or we'll be here all day) and we ended up in France. In my true form, I'm an elite-looking praying mantis, with three eyes. Really if you saw me in true life form, you would think I'm totally awesome looking. I know it sounds a little odd having three eyes, but well, it's not. Anyhow, Ralb and I tried to get back home because we could only stay on Earth for a certain amount of time, so we hitched a ride on Suzzy's spaceship. Talk about a small world. She was the Suzz who Ralb had fallen in love with in Bedrocktown (which I have to tell you made me want to gag more than once, and with praying mantis roots, I have a strong stomach). She changed her name, her accent, and her chest size and became the latest and hottest pop star. I found it fascinating so much could happen in such a short period of time while we were in France, but something about time-traveling and math, and well, I admit that's not my strong suit. ANYWAY, getting back to Suzz. Well, TZZ (yes, that TZZ) wanted to launch her into space for advertising, to do a reality show based on our little chickie poo.

Long story shorter, Alvin the security guard spilled tea on the controls and instead of launching into space, we ended up in New Zealand.

I wasn't too miffed mind you. It's par for the three-dinner course with Ralb, my brother, at the helm, we wouldn't end up where we'd wanted to go. I'd always wanted to see New Zealand, visit with the dingoes and the Kangaroos (who knew that was Australia—certainly not me). I thought all those places down under were the same.

That just about brings us up to today.

Oh right, I did save the world from a massive oil spill, thanks to my (insert cough here) brains and quick thinking, but I'm not one to brag.

Not much.

So after spending the spaceship ride alternating between being stuck in a cupboard with a life raft and in a hot guy's space suit pocket, who btw, wasn't Josh, this was preferably more comfortable.

Okay, I admit it.

I'm majorly fickle.

Chapter 2

"Should this be our last hand?" I innocently asked Freaky Freddie. Hey, it was his idea to play Strip Poker, can I help it if I'm beating the pants off him?

He mumbled something which I didn't quite catch but I'm sure would be bleeped out in any PG movie.

"Folks, please ensure your seatbelts are fastened and your seats are in an upright position." An authoritative voice came over the loudspeaker. A pretty flight attendance, wearing skin-tight blue pants and a white blouse which she must have got on sale because there weren't any buttons, and she needed a scarf to hide her bits, tidied up our garbage. I admired the way she adverted her eyes to his lack of clothes. She must really like her job.

"Hey," I smiled the smile of the innocent. "Isn't the reason you got those chest tat's was to show them off?" While I wasn't a fan of inking, I did like the details the artist had provided. Who would have thought a seahorse and mermaid would have so much in common? I mean to have an entire underwater world across your biceps, trailing down to your belly button (which was now the Jewel of Neptune). Past the nether regions, seaweed traveling down each leg where fish hid was truly a work of art. Okay, maybe it wasn't a major work of art, but there's a critic in every bar.

"You lied to me," he hissed, as my zipped

sweatshirt covered his, well, you know.

"I honestly have never played this game before," I admitted. Okay, we had a similar game on Zorca-twenty-three called Antenna Flush and I was the reigning Antenna Queen, but I wasn't about to tell him that.

"Come on, be a sport!" I tossed him his clothes. Frankly, the sight of him almost naked was turning my stomach and I really didn't want Freaky Freddie as an enemy. He was a member of the most popular rock band on your planet and I wasn't about to cut off my nose to spit on my face. "Let's say we have one more hand and winner takes all." I quickly retracted that statement when I saw the way his eyes lit up. "I mean, the winner of this hand is the overall winner and has bragging rights to say they won at this silly game." What can I say? My Parental Being taught me a thing or two about being magnanimous. I guess you could say she didn't raise no fool and I didn't know if I would ever need anything from Freaky Freddie or Jocko for that matter.

I dealt the cards, the occupants of the plane were quiet, and you could hear the wheels drop as I picked up my cards and watched his face. Like a country and western song, you had to know when to hang onto them, know when to get rid of them and I breathed in trying to appear nonchalant.

I was holding a royal frigging flush. I had the best hand I had all night and what did I do. I played the cards very wisely.

I admit it. I couldn't help myself. I was competitive, right from the get-go. I couldn't help it. On Zorca-twenty-three I have over six hundred siblings, so one tends to be a little aggressive. A grin passed over my face and when I glanced up at Ralb, he shook his head like a dog at the water trough.

Right! I had to play smart, not nice. I couldn't gloat. I had to be the mature one here. I mean, here I was fully clothed, save for my sweatshirt where Freaky Freddie sat across from me, with all but his family jewels on display, and they were hidden by my sweater. Which by the by, he was so keeping.

"Do you need any cards?" I asked, picking up the lingo like I was a Vegas dealer. All that was missing was a green visor and I was GtoG.

"Give me one," he said, confidence creeping into his voice like a cat on a warm windowsill.

"Fine." I dealt out the cards and gave myself three. Yep, you read right. I gave myself three. I ditched the perfect royal flush and picked up three cards, keeping my fingers and everything else crossable I would get lousy cards.

Geez a murphy, when it's your night, it's your night.

"Show me what you've got," Freaky Freddie said, jumping up in his seat so fast, he almost dislodged the sweatshirt. I so didn't want to see what women across the Atlantic and Pacific were clamoring for.

I laid down my cards like I was on my way to a funeral. Which in fact I was.

Mine.

I'd picked up two queens, and I now had three of a kind.

"Yes!" He leaped up, pumped his fist in the air and I ladylike adverted my eyes. I had to look at his cards, in disbelief.

Staring up at me were four aces and a ten.

"Yes! Freaky Freddie rocks! I so beat you! I so beat you!" He jumped across the aisle, his left hand firmly covering himself as he high-fived Jocko, the flight attendant, and everyone else in the immediate vicinity.

"Yes, you sure did," I admitted, covering the smirk on my face. Ralb gave a sigh of relief so loud he blocked out the sounds of the jet engines breaking.

Bracing myself against the back of the plush seat, I automatically placed my feet on the floor as if the movement would help the plane slow down. I hated this part, hated not being in control of my fate. Having to rely on the mysterious voice who said calming words, but I happened to see when he headed to the loo and he didn't look like he was old enough to drive a car, never mind a machine which flies fast, high and had the power to kill at a moment's notice.

I clapped. Okay, it was like a cheesy movie where the guy got the girl, but I couldn't help myself. I was so relieved to be back on Earth after our gazillion hour flight from New Zealand to England.

"Good day, mates! Welcome to Gatwick, where the temperature is a balmy twenty degrees with a slight drizzle," the Captain said joyously.

See, I told you the guy was a young'un. How can anyone be thrilled when the temperature is freezing? We'd just traveled from NZ, where it was winter and now we were in England, where it's always raining. Planet traveling sure sucked the big one.

"Great! I didn't bring a coat and much as I hate to ask for it, is there any way I can get my sweatshirt back?" My Parental Being had told me before I left

Zorca-twenty-three to pack a coat, but really who listens to their Parental Being. Not me, and I'm sure you have your moments as well too. Am I right? I tried to avoid eye contact with Freaky Freddie, but I couldn't. I couldn't help but laugh. Here was a guy who was on the cover of Persone Magazine as one of the world's sexiest bachelors, and he was standing in front of me, finally fully dressed. With his famous come hither look gleaming from his lake blue-colored eyes, I couldn't resist grinning. He'd gotten dressed in a matter of minutes; how he managed to complete the feat with his seat belt remaining on was a sight to behold, but I had to laugh because his T-shirt was on backward, the label facing toward the front which caused even Hildy to snort.

"Sure, it's not the first time it's happened, Freaky Freddie, but you would have done a better job dressing in the dark," Hildy mumbled.

Whipping off the shirt, he quickly flipped it around and put it back on. "I would have done fine, but I was the victim of a major cheater." He reached over and pulled my ear.

I'd like to have said it was done with affection, but to be completely honest, it hurt like the devil.

"Hey, Freaky Freddie," Jocko scolded, his blond moussed hair standing on point. "Never bet what you can't afford to lose." He patted Suzz on the arm with a major degree of ownership. "Now make up and let's get off this tin can and teach these foreigners a thing or two about bangers and mash."

Great! I was in a strange country, with my brother and Suzz for protection and now I was going to be sacrificed into some weird offering.

Chapter 3

We flew right through Customs, which at Gatwick was undergoing some sort of major construction renovation. I guess that's a poor choice of words since we recently deplaned, so I'll reword it to we walked quickly through Customs. And I have to say I was majority disappointed. The place was royally messy. There were caution tape, ladders, and paint cans scattered across the walkways.

Not that I expected to be greeted by any of the Royals, though it would have been nice. I mean, I am a guest in their country and when I was in New Zealand there were Royal faces on the money, so I did feel like we were friends, but whatev. But to be met with fat men in hard hats, it was hardly the stuff dreams are made of, even if they did whistle at me and show me their butkis when they bent over.

I did feel like royalty though when I walked through the airport and we had to dodge the screaming girls to find our black limo. Those girls could really scream, and I could be wrong, but I think I saw one of them faint. I wanted to go and help her, but Freaky Freddie had such a firm grip of my arm I couldn't stop.

"She'll get the help she needs," he hissed into my ear. "Don't stop or we'll be mobbed."

I thought the point of being rich and famous was having the ability to help others, but then again what did I know. I was just a mere space-traveling Alien who was neither rich nor famous but did like to help.

Pushed inside a limo, again I was awestruck with the extravagant lifestyles of the rich and famous. I was sitting with my back to the driver, a fat armrest beside me. When Jocko encouraged me to open it, I found a mini bar filled with soda and chips. My finger found a button and pushed it, revealing more booze bottles than I'd seen in any liquor store.

"Pour me a gin and tonic, sugar plum fairy," Freaky Freddie ordered.

I guess all was forgiven with the strip poker fiasco as now I was his server. I so would not get the man anything, and before I could retort, Ralb spoke for me.

"She'd be happy too. Anybody else want anything?"

Great! I got busy pouring drinks, adding ice and tonic not to mention handing out bags and packages of chips and pretzels. Cripes, I was like the flight attendant without the pay or the plane. And I was completely missing the passing scenery.

How cool was it the cars drive on the wrong side of the road to the United States? And everyone seemed to know they were supposed to.

British flags flew on every flagpole and as we entered downtown London, we ended up on a circle where all the cars seemed to go around and around and around, before shooting off in different directions.

"How much longer?" Jocko asked as he hit another button lowering the glass between us and the driver.

"Not long now, mate. Probably with the traffic, we're looking at another half hour, or forty-five." The driver's accent sing-songed the news, but his head was wrapped in a giant blue bandage. I hope he didn't hurt himself driving. He had such a pretty voice; he could tell me I only had six months to live, and I would be okay with it. Well, not literally, well, you know what I mean.

I rolled down the window to inhale the smells of my new city. I leaned out the window and passed a dog in another car doing the same thing. Breathing deeply, I smelt exhaust fumes, carbon fumes, and the smell of wet socks, no doubt from all the rain the country receives.

"Roll up the window bird, don't want to get the inside all wet." Jocko had a drink in one hand, which seemed to have evaporated in a matter of minutes, and his other on Suzz's knee. Ralb seemed to be taking it okay his former girlfriend and first Earth femawl was now chatting up another mawl. He kept his eyes firmly focused out the window, seeming to ignore what was going on right beside him.

I put the window up and as we whizzed by castles, I'd only seen in pictures and on my *wad*. It amazed me there was any rock at all left in England with all the ones used to make dwellings and fences. We passed a soccer field where two teams were fighting over one black-and-white ball. Really, wouldn't it be fairer if they each had their own ball? Seems to me it would be a lot friendlier too.

Finally, we reached downtown London.

Despite the disagreement I knew I'd have to listen to, I once again put down the window and gazed up at the London Eye, a Ferris wheel-type contraption which was so high I'm sure on a clear day you could see the Eiffel Tower in Paris.

"There's MI-6," Jocko pointed out a brown brick building right on the river. "Home to our famous spies."

I knew he was making that up and I bet the building he pointed out was really a bank or something. That's why it had all the cameras around it. Geez, he was a rotten tour guide.

Double-decker buses competed with black taxis in lanes that didn't appear wide enough for a bicycle. And the pedestrians did more jay walking than any bird I'd ever seen. They crossed streets without a glance or acknowledgment of any on-coming traffic. I held my breath more than once as our driver navigated around the obstacles.

"Can we see England Palace?" I asked, keen to see any royalty. I'd seen a copy of *Halo Magazine* and knew that royalty in this country were a dime a dozen and I'd be falling over all kinds of the upper class of British monarchy. I guess if the major royals couldn't spare a cup of tea for me, I'd have to settle for some lesser royals.

"You just did," Jocko smirked.

"What?" I flung my head around looking backward or rather forward, depending on how you were facing. "There's nothing back there but a statue and a big white industrial building." I punched him in the shoulder and smirked right back at him when he cringed in pain. "You think you can put one over on the tourist, don't you? I know what England Place looks like and that's not it," I recited from a recent article I'd read. "England Palace has been the home of kings and queens for over five hundred years. During World War Two, the king and queen stayed in the castle, despite the fact German bombs were dropping overhead. In fact, it was bombed nine times and yet only one person was killed. Many monarchs would run to hide out in the countryside, but they remained in London. Needless to say, this endeared them to the population and encouraged the Allies to fight even more against the enemy. And another fun fact, the palace contains over forty thousand light bulbs. I bet they have a guy whose only job it is to change them."

I was the one who should be the tour guide. Maybe while I was here, I could get a part-time job teaching tourists about the country. Or from the sounds of things, teaching some of the natives as well.

"Thank you, Miss Walking Encyclopedia." Freaky Freddie raised his eyebrows and rolled his eyes heavenward. "Now that we've all had our history lesson for let's just say the entire year, can we decide what we're going to do as soon as we get to the flat?"

"Well, excuse me for trying to educate you and get you folks excited about something other than the dreaded bangers and mash." As soon as the words were out of my mouth, I covered my hands over my pie hole and wanted to take back everything I'd ever said, including the part about the palace stuff. I was a total moron, a total alien moron. Why, oh why, did I bring up the weird British ritual again? Would I never learn?

Especially when I saw drool drip from the corner of Jocko's lips.

Yikes, I was about to become his dinner, supper, or whatever the heck they called it over here.

Chapter 4

"Here we are, mate," the taxi driver chirped when he pulled the car to a stop in front of a seven-story building.

The trunk popped open. I alighted from the car, stumbling over the uneven cobblestone sidewalk.

"Careful, sugar plum fairy. You're stepping across the oldest walkway in London. Rumor has it, it was built by the conquering Romans as they headed toward Bath," Freaky Freddie lectured.

"Wow, and you called her the walking encyclopedia." Suzz laughed, picking up her matching pink Louis Voot suitcase and carry on. I was surprised. I thought for sure she'd wait until someone picked it up for her, but the girl continued to amaze me. "Can we get up to the flat? I have to have a major pee."

You could give the girl fancy luggage, but she was still a potty mouth girl. Not that our Suzz, aka Suzzy, was from the wrong side of the tracks at all. In fact, she was from the rich side of Bedrocktown. But she still had an uncouth mouth and no high-class upbringing would be able to rid her of it. Believe me, I tried to get her to talk ladylike, but it was a losing battle.

"Follow me, people." Jocko ordered as he punched in a four-digit code, and the door opened. "Get ready for a hike, folks."

We walked up a set of twelve steps and then hit a

landing where there was a closed door. But he didn't stop at the door, or the landing, but continued upwards. For eight more sets of stairs and landings.

Oh my gosh, I was going to die for sure. I was totally out of breath, so much so I felt as if I was in a marathon without the water breaks.

"Can't you guys afford an elevator?" I asked when I grabbed the railing to stop myself from tumbling backward. I wasn't an expert, but I don't think they were that expensive to install and I'd been on one with my BFF Nicola. Once I got over the fact I was going to plumage to my death, I enjoyed the experience, somewhat. At least better than what I was going through now. My heart was beating so fast, I thought at one point it was going to pop out right through my shirt.

"We didn't want to ruin the authenticity of the building. It survived WWII and I think it should be able to survive a chart-topping band." Jocko smirked.

What is it with this guy? It was like he was either scowling or smirking. I'd definitely have to work to increase his repertoire of facial expressions.

"Why? Do The Bees live here?" I asked, innocently. I knew which band he was referring to, but I wasn't about to give him a bigger ego than he already had. I already knew I'd have a hard time getting his head through any regular sized door.

The remark was met with a scowl. Are you surprised? I know I wasn't. This time Ralb shared Jocko's expression. Was the look contagious? Was my brother catching the evil mean look as well?

Cautiously I moved away from the door; I didn't want to catch anything either one of them might have.

"Give the bird a break," Freaky Freddie ordered.

Obviously, the brains in the band, he knew when to push someone's buttons and when to drop the subject, though he should have learned that lesson himself before he'd lost all his clothes. "We're here." He keyed in a pin number and the door opened.

From the dingy hallway which had only lit up when we'd approached the magic light, it was like entering Aladdin's cave. Everywhere I looked was gold or at least the color of it. Overhead hung a magnificent chandelier with twenty-seven arms pointed out in different directions, each with a sixty-watt bulb attached. It lit up every corner of the room. When I saw the vaulted ceiling, I admit I staggered backward. Lush trees, plants, and foliage abounded in the background, more shades of green than I'd ever seen used anywhere in nature. Xron, an elder from my planet showed me his tree pot before I left on my travels; the fullness of the trees reminded me of Zorca-twenty-three's version of heaven. Nestled in all the greenery were naked and nearly nude angels, with the bodies of goddesses, positioned around two males lounging on red velvet cushions with Jocko's and Freaky Freddie's faces.

"Ralb, look at these paintings." I stood still, getting a slight kink in my neck as I looked skyward and blinked with surprise.

"Where's Hildy?" I asked to cover my astonishment at the artwork if one could call it that. I wondered if I'd get to meet the artist because I'd like to interrogate them to find out where they got their inspiration. It was like they'd traveled to Zorca-twenty-three or saw inside a crystal ball as to what was going on at home.

"Right behind you."

"No, I mean, she's missing from the band pictures. Jocko's there and so's Freaky Freddie, but I don't see Hildy anywhere." I peered more intently into the dome to see if I could locate her, maybe I'd missed her the first time, but it didn't take a detective to determine she wasn't there.

"She was the painter," Jocko admitted. "That's how we met."

Hildy jumped in and explained, "I answered an advertisement in the paper for a ceiling painter. After I read it, I thought what type of loser would put in such an ad, so it was more curiosity than anything else that led me to answer it. I rang them, set up an appointment and the rest is history as they say."

I vowed to ask her more questions, but I had to wait for a more opportune time. She knew about our planet and I had to find out how and why.

"Everyone grab a bedroom and if there's not enough to go around, well, I for one will be willing to share," Freaky Freddie leered.

I grabbed my bag and sprinted faster than I ever had in my life toward the bedroom wing of the flat. You might wonder how I knew where I was heading, but it was like I had an internal GPS system. I zeroed in on the wing and ran through an open door, put my case down on a blue velveteen canopied bed, and pumped my fist in the air

"*Yes!*" I was so sleeping alone during this stint of my Earth voyage. I flopped down on the double bed and checked out the room. Decorated in yellow flowered wallpaper, a dark cherry wood fireplace covered one entire wall, topped with a gigantic mirror which reflected the other side of the mammoth room.

Ornaments decorated the mantel, a clock with cherubs contorting up the sides, candlesticks which I'm assuming were purposeful in case the power went out, and two little boxes. Curiosity got the better of me and I couldn't resist opening them. The first contained match sticks, and the second candles. Geez, how disappointing. I was expecting something really exciting, like jewels or at least some kind of treasure. Next to the fireplace was a feeble writing table and chair. I definitely wouldn't be sitting on it anytime soon. It looked like it would fall apart if I breathed on it the wrong way,

A loveseat in the shape of a sideways "S" was tucked in a corner. Pictures of old people covered each of the walls and I fully expected the eyes to follow me around the room like I'd seen in a horror movie but before I could test them, I was interrupted by repetitive coughing.

I got up and closed the door of *my* room. I opened my suitcase and out popped major attitude.

"Could you not have gotten me out any faster? I could have suffocated in there and then once again I'd be dead and you'd be responsible," Rotsen nagged me.

In case you missed the earlier description of him, in my other two adventures, Rotsen is my dandelion who is in need of a major attitude adjustment. He likes to impersonate accents and gives me major trouble, but he does have my back and he's saved my back bacon more than once. And I must say I did return the favor by saving his life.

I know the scales aren't really balanced between us, but I was glad he was in the owzies category rather than me. Besides, between you and me, if it wasn't for the *mist book* I wouldn't have had a clue how to save his life. Luckily, I'd found the ingredients I needed when we were in New Zealand and he was GtoG, if a little woozy in the aftermath.

I have to tell you a *mist book* is the one thing you want to have with you when you're interplanetary traveling. It came through for us when I saved Bedrocktown from E. coli poisoning and it also helped us when we needed passports in a hurry.

"Hello, we're talking," Rotsen admonished me. "Can you come back from dreamland and focus here?" He inchworm walked towards the window and stuck his petals between the window blinds. "Take a gander out here. It's like we're on the back lot for Kono Street."

I couldn't help giggling. My dandelion was a huge soap opera fan and it didn't matter if we were in the United States, New Zealand, Australia, or Britain, he snuck in his *wad* and watched the telly. He could hold his own in conversation with any soap opera-aholic.

"Rotsen, the ceiling artwork is of a tree pot forest." I winced, knowing the reaction I was going to receive.

"Sure, it is." Rotsen folded over his leaves and sighed heavily. "Man, what I wouldn't give to have a normal travel companion." He twisted his head around and peered at the mantel clock.

"Rotsen, it's up to me to get us home. Ralb has turned over the power to me," I bragged. I saved a town from E. coli poisoning and penguins from an oil spill, how hard can it be to get two people and a dandelion back to our home planet? Should be a piece of cheese!

"How about you bring me back a cuppa and I'll settle in here and watch Kono Street?" He untwisted himself from the blinds and headed toward the set of chairs. He flopped down and with his *wad* fine-tuned it until he got the appropriate channel. "All is good with the world. But what is it with these people? Why can't they get their acts together?"

"Alrighty then. I'll head down to the kitchen and get a cup of tea! That is if I don't get abducted by aliens and taken to a far remote planet where I get probed for my knowledge. We know how some of those aliens like to probe a little too deeply." Actually, it so wasn't true, and from the nod and the smile on his petals, I wasn't sure if he'd heard me or not. Such is our relationship. It could kind of be described as love/hate.

I pulled the door shut and left Rotsen with his addiction. At this rate, I was going to be on Dr. Shell, running an intervention. But that would have to wait as my stomach's rumbling reminded me, I hadn't had anything to eat since New Zealand. I couldn't eat on the plane. Something about tumbling toward my death from a high altitude did little to make me hungry. But now I was on terra firma and I was starving.

I followed my nose, not that it was big or anything, but it did have a good sense of smell. Sizzling and splattering accompanied a fantastic aroma. The frying pan seemed to have a life of its own as sausages crackled in the oil.

Freaky Freddie stood over the pan like an orchestra director, turning the food a quarter of an inch every few seconds.

"I hope everyone brought their hunger on," he said, "there are bangers on their way, and I have some potatoes I'm cooking up to mash."

"Sorry, don't you mean potatoes, not potatoes?" I

asked with my emphasis on the toes not on the ta.

"You are a card," Jocko bellowed across the room as he stepped into the walk-in fridge and emerged with a beer. "Hildy, want a brewski? You're too young, April."

Hildy shook her head and headed to the sink where she filled up the kettle, then plugged it in. There was something in her slow movements which concerned me. There definitely was something off with this girl and I meant to find out what it was and in the not-too-distant future.

Freaky Freddie turned off the gas, and then using tongs lifted each of the sausages out of the pan and onto a paper towel-lined plate, the grease raced through the towel like a race car towards the finish line.

Chatter filled the air with such nonsense topics as the score of the latest soccer game, which I think the British call football, and how their team—apparently the boys owned them—the Rugby Rashers was going to do in the semi-finals.

Ralb stared out the window, and I moved to his side to see what had caught his attention. The street came to life as the garage doors covering the windows of the stores were opened. Fish and chip stores nestled alongside betting stores. In fact, when I moved closer to my brother, I counted seven betting places in a single block. I wonder what the odds would be of us getting home with my help. Low I bet. No lie. I guess there was more than a passing interest for the British and their sports.

"Are you okay?" I asked, whispering to him, not wanting to embarrass him in front of people we really didn't know. I mean, if I'm going to embarrass him, I'd like to at least do it in front of people who are going to appreciate it.

"What?" he asked snarkily.

"Geez! I just wanted to make sure you were okay! You seem a little quiet and to be honest, I'm a little concerned."

"How can I not be okay? We're relying on you to get us home, the same person who claimed to be all lovely dovey with Josh when kissing another mawl. Talk about fickle."

In my defense, I was trying to get Josh back to my planet, so I could get him revived. I admit I used the oldest trick in the *mist book* to accomplish what needed to get done. "Really, Ralb, get over it. In case you forgot, we've been on Earth for close to our maximum amount of time and we're going to explode if we don't get home soon." Okay, I was exaggerating about the exploding part but only slightly. At least that's what I thought would happen. When I last saw my handler, he explained to me that we could only stay on Earth for a maximum of six months, and in an indirect way told me my mawl Parental Being was in fact an Earthling. How's that for a Jerry Winter show?

I, of course, was too clueless, or in my own defense I was excited about interplanetary traveling to remember much and he could have told me my relative was a famous humanoid and it wouldn't have registered.

"Ralb?" I asked directly. "Do you know what will happen if we don't make it back to Zorca-twenty-three before our time's up?"

"You mean you don't know?" He laughed so loud, everyone in the room stopped talking.

"What's so funny?" Freaky Freddie asked. I turned and saw a major kitchen instrument in his hand and was relieved to see him pop it into the pot instead of using it as a weapon. Not that he appeared to need an anger management course or anything, but you never knew with these rock stars. Anything and everything might set them off.

"Oh, nothing really, just a family joke," Ralb said, gripping my arm tightly and leaning into my ear. "Nothing major really, just you change once and for all into an ananoid, no changing back with or without pills."

There was no way I was going to become an ananoid permanently. For one thing, it seemed really painful, and for another, it was just totally gross. I kinda liked being your type of humanoid. I'd much rather be a humanoid femawl, with the option of having a car door being opened for me, a dinner being paid for and flowers being brought to me. Not that any of those things have ever happened to me. I've never been on a proper Earth date to be honest, though I have left a party with Josh and we did kiss, but it wasn't like it was planned or anything. At least by me.

"I'd better make sure we get home in time," I hissed back at him.

"Oas, this should be interesting to watch." He smiled. "If we time it right at the summer solstice, we can use the rocks to get home." He held up his hands. "But I'm not about to tell you how to do it. I'm sure you can figure it all out on your own."

"If you folks are done with your sibling whisper fest why not come over here and we'll have a quick brunch?" Jocko asked as he watched Hildy place plates and silverware on the table. It was kind of cool how every place setting had a hot mat beneath it. "Suzz is sleeping, so I'll save some for her."

At each place was a teacup and a little plate underneath it. It was interesting how Hildy made the tea. It didn't involve the simple act of placing a tea bag on a string in a hot pot of water. Heck no! She poured loose tea leaves into a metal container and then poured water over top of it. Then as a weird act, she dumped the tea leaves into the cup.

"When you finish your tea, I'll read your leaves," she advised. Personally, I think it's a lot more interesting to read a good book—I especially like the ones called Chick Lit, or Rom-Com but whatever floats her boat.

"Gee, I can't wait," I tried to sound enthusiastic, but it didn't sit right somehow. I took my time eating, not wanting to be the first to finish and therefore the first in line for the freak side show. "Can I have another sausage?" The spices exploding in my mouth were to die for. How had I lived so long without tasting a sausage? I asked, not caring if I looked like a piglet, especially alongside Hildy who didn't eat enough to feed a parakeet, and even Jocko who picked at his food. Did they know something I didn't? Did Freaky Freddie plan on poisoning us and then cutting up our bodies into little pieces before anyone noticed us missing? Okay, I admit I had a vivid imagination, and it didn't help I saw Freaky Freddie watching a biography show on famous British murderers on the plane, while he wanted me to watch the clouds. Sounds mighty suspicious if you ask me, which I know you didn't, but I think I'd have to get back to Rotsen and let him know if I went missing who the culprit would be.

"Okay, I'll do April first. Finish up your tea," Hildy ordered me like she was a drill sergeant in the army and I the new recruit. "Hurry up! Hurry up!"

I burnt my tongue, then the back of my throat in my haste to get the drink down. I pierced another of the sausages, the grease jumping up and squirting me right in the eye. I wiped it with the paper towel Hildy had conveniently placed beside my plate. Determined not to have the food attack me again, I poked my fork through the rest of the rolled meat. I saw how Jocko did it, dipping a piece of sausage into the mashed potato mountains and then popped it into his mouth. Yum. I could see how this could become a national treasure. Never mind royalty and all the history. If you ever get to England, you must sample the bangers and mash.

"Would you hurry up?" Hildy hissed.

I gulped down the rest and slammed the cup onto its tiny little plate. "Fine, here you go." I hoped my snarky attitude would get her goat but obviously not as she reached over and pulled the cup and saucer towards herself. "Is your crystal ball in the other room?"

Wow, the look I got would stop and peel wallpaper off the wall, so evil her face looked with her now squinted eyes and her mouth in a tight line.

She swirled the remaining liquid around, then used the towel and placed it over the top of the teacup. She turned it upside down, and the tea was soaked up into the towel.

"Okay, let's see here." She tilted the cup to the left, then the right, then back to the left again.

"This is real stimulating," Ralb said, from his seat beside Hildy. "What do you do for an encore? Cut a man in half?"

"Yes, matter of fact I do, and I have the perfect assistant, Ralb!"

I choked back laughter as Ralb's face went even whiter than normal.

"Sorry, I'm busy." He folded and refolded his napkin, avoiding eye contact with anyone and everyone at the table.

"And on that note, can we continue with our show?" Jocko scowled.

Freaky Freddie got up and began to clear the table. He scrapped all the left-over food on the plates into the sink, then pulled open a door and loaded them onto racks. That was a great way to put them away. I really don't know why anyone would need so many cupboards.

"I see travel in your future," the all-knowing Hildy said.

Like no kidding, we just got off a plane and we had to go to the States for a concert, crossing the pond as the Brits like to say. Then there was always my interplanetary travel, but we so weren't going to go there or cross that bridge.

"Good thing my passport is new," I joked to relieve the tension in the room. See, that's the problem with these gurus, you can always read more into what they say and interrupt it in many different ways.

"Umm, I don't know how to tell you this." She slammed the cup down onto the table, almost causing it to shatter. "Never mind, we're done for the night. I'm heading up to bed."

"Come on, you have to tell me what you saw!" I waved my hands around like I was a magician. "Please oh wise one, tell us what you saw in my tea leaves." I had to stop from laughing. "Let me guess, you see romance in my future." I could only hope.

"Actually, no." She paused before gathering up the mess on the table. "Do you really want to know?"

"Yeah, of course I do. Tell us!!" Duh, like of course we want to know. But maybe that was all part of the game, you know just like on the telly when they're about to tell the audience who the murderer is and what happens.... they break for a commercial.

"Okay, you asked for it. I don't really feel right about telling you this, but I see Death and you in jail."

A shiver ricocheted down my spine and I shivered uncontrollably. Have to admit I didn't see that one coming?

Chapter 5

"Rotsen, she said I was going to go end up behind bars and that there was Death in my future." I grabbed another of the three pillows already under my head on the bed and shoved another one to boost up my head even further. Rain thumped against the windowpane matching my depressed mood. "There's not too many ways you can take that the wrong way."

I waited for the voice of reason to speak. I knew he'd make it all better. He'd solved all my problems since I landed on this stupid planet and I knew in my heart of hearts, that he'd help me through this one. Ralb wasn't about to do anything. Right now, he was playing pool with Jocko and Freaky Freddie. Geez, bro, thanks for your concern. Maybe you can bake me a cake with a file in it when I'm in the slammer, provided you sink the eight ball first.

I so couldn't be behind bars. I was claustrophobic and I didn't sleep well on beds with thin mattresses. I needed more than one pillow. I know that's strange coming from a previous praying mantis. You'd think we'd be happy to sleep anywhere and any place, but to be honest, I've gotten kind of used to the luxuries in life, and a good night's sleep was one of them. And I had a delicate stomach. Right now, the grease from the bangers and mash was whipping around my stomach like they were competing in a sword fight.

"Well, it doesn't sound good or promising." Rotsen shrugged his petals. "You sure get yourself into some pickles."

I sat up. "What do you mean me?" I stuttered. "All I did was have my stupid tea leaves read by some second-rate soothsayer."

"Hold the phone." He held up his leaves like he was a traffic cop. "I only said…."

"I heard what you said, and thanks loads for helping me," I whined, and my tear ducts filled. "All I want to do is go home."

A knock at the door interrupted my tirade. Like my hands were on fire, I shoved Rotsen under the pillows and if anyone accused me of being somewhat rough with the dandelion, I think I was justified. But I would still deny it.

"Who's there?" You can't be too careful letting people into your room. I'd seen way too many horror movies on my *wad* where the innocent sorority student lets in the 'friend' only to be bludgeoned to death.

"It's me, Hildy."

Okay, now I had a dilemma. Do I let her in, or should I ignore her? Pretend I wasn't here.

"You can't pretend you're not here, you already answered her," a muffled voice said from under the pillows.

I jumped back onto the bed, crossed my walking sticks, and put a bit more pressure than necessary on the headboard-slash-pillows. "Enter!"

She strutted into the room like Suzzy on a red carpet and pushing my walking sticks aside sat down on my bed. "What do you want?" I asked, picking at my fingernail. "Don't you think you've done enough damage here?"

"Hey, I was just having some fun. I didn't mean anything by it," Hildy laughed. "I should have known better. You never could take a joke."

"Yeah, right and you know that how? Because of the small amount of time, we spent together on the plane." What was it with this chick? She was a complete head case. Acting like we were all BFF's, that we had history. Please, you had to work a little harder than that to become a friend of mine. I was mighty choosey, even if you might not think so with having a dandelion for a traveling companion.

"You mean you don't know?" Hurt raced across her face, stopping at the tear duct tattoo, her left eye dropping a little bit. "I thought you would have guessed it by now." She reached across and brushed my bangs out of my eyes. "I'm disappointed Rotsen didn't figure it out by now. I always thought between him, Ralb, and you, he was the brains of the operation."

Stunned, I continued to stare at her. "How do you know Rotsen?"

Shuffling, rumbling, and mumbling went on under my head and Rotsen poked his head out from the jumble of pillows.

"Gorget, how did you get here?" Rotsen asked, his petals crossed, and I knew from his stance, he'd be jumping into his favorite karate move if the situation arose. He so had my back.

"Gorget?" I was shocked to say the least and I fell back against the pillows.

Gorget was Hildy. Hildy was Gorget.

The last time I'd seen this two-timing (that I knew of, there were probably more) mawl, he'd been snuggling up to Kaj (my former BAF—Best Ananoid Friend) on Zorca-twenty-three. He'd ordered me—you read it right, ordered me—not to go to Earth. Just the fact he told me I couldn't do something made me want to do it all the more. Where did he get off telling me not to? It wasn't like we were married or anything. I fumed again just remembering our last conversation.

"You got it in one, babe." His hand lingered over mine, and he lightly rubbed the top in the way familiar to my Zorcan-twenty-three form. "I couldn't wait until you came home, so I came to see you."

"That's why the toilet seat was up," I said. I explained to Rotsen who gave me a questioning look. "When we were on the plane, I used the bathroom right after Hildy, er, whatever you're calling yourself this week."

"Go on!" Rotsen urged, knowing how I tend to easily get off topic.

"When I went into the bathroom, the toilet seat was up. A femawl earthling puts the seat down to sit on it, but a mawl puts the seat up, so when he's urinating it doesn't get on the seat." See, I have learned a few things in my travels. But I had more important issues to cover and I had to know the answers. Or more like I deserved to know the answers.

"How?" I yanked my hand away and child-like I hid it under the duvet. Just in case he decided to reach across and pull at my other one, I hid it too. "How did you get here?"

"You have Kaj to thank for that." He walked toward the end of the bed and began to stroke the wooden pole holding up the material roof of the bed. "You know how she became a Chuckwalla lizard when you saw her on the rocket ship."

I nodded, afraid to speak for fear I'd say something I'd regret.

"Well, it was a plan we hatched up together. She always wanted to see the worlds and I agreed that it would be something fun to do together."

Rotsen popped a leaf over my mouth, but I forcibly removed it. "How come you encourage, no wait, I think a better word is allow her to see the worlds and me you gave a major hard time about wanting to travel to Earth to save my brother?"

"What can I say?" He waved his arms. "I had a change of heart. I saw the light so to speak." He shrugged again. "I saw a poster that said, if you *jobe* something, say bye-bye like you mean it."

"Oh please!"

He misinterpreted my words as obvious encouragement for he continued. "I felt really bad about the way things were left with us and I wanted to make amends." He ran his fingers down the rivets in the wood before continuing. "I talked Kaj into turning herself into a lizard, not much of a stretch…" He grinned when he saw I nodded. "And then I was in the cage as a dead rat."

Not much of a stretch there either.

"That was you?" Rotsen asked, inviting himself into our conversation. "I've never seen such a big ugly old varmint."

Surprisingly Gorget took that as a compliment.

"You know Kaj hates you now."

"Yeah, on that note, thanks so much." He rushed to continue as if to sense I was getting ticked off. "So, Josh became human again and Kaj changed as well into a super tall humanoid with braids down her back. Where she got that idea from I'll never know?"

"Maybe she was trying to be your dream girl, knowing how you used to drool over those supermodels you watched on your *wad*." I remember more than once when we were dating, he'd be late because he had to watch the end of some pageant on his *wad.*

"Yeah, that's probably why she put in the request before you made her change her mind about me." Gorget shrugged.

"You're such a mawl," I said, totally exasperated with him and the conversation. I could shake myself when I think of the sleepless nights I spent dreaming of this ananoid. Total waste of time.

"You have to admit you were impressed by my painting! I saw the way you almost drooled when you saw the tree pots!" Hildy/Gorget bragged.

"How did you manage to do it so fast?" I asked, surprising myself by actually being curious. "You were with us in New Zealand, yet Jocko and Freaky Freddie gave the impression that you've been with them forever."

"Gotta thank the latest edition of the *mist book,* yours is sooo out of date." He laughed. "It does come in handy. I used the forward/forward/reaching event where the intended victim loses concept of time. What is actually mere minutes, is years and years to the victim." He shrugged again. "Also, a quick paint by numbers on the ceiling and we were GtoG."

"But how did you get to Earth in the first place?" I asked. "I know you weren't on my asteroid."

I was ready to slap him when he shrugged. "It's a long, boring story as to how I became a femawl. Let's just say, the writers of the *mist book* have a wicked sense of humor."

Rotsen burst out laughing. "Are you saying you fell for the recipe on page seventy-two where if you mix water from a goldfish bowl and seeds from an evergreen tree together on the night of a full moon, you'll become irresistible to women."

"I think you must have misread it somewhere along the line. I found Hildy, er you, to be quite intimidating and not very approachable."

Rotsen was still laughing, so hard in fact, he had to use his leaf to wipe away the tears from his stamen. "He read it as water from a goldfish bowl, not water from a gold-colored fishbowl." Rotsen held up a leaf expecting me to high-five him. "Totally my idea for that one. I thought it would separate the wheat from the chaff, so to speak."

"I should have known it would have something to do with you." Gorget/Hildy looked like he was going to punch Rotsen and that was something I for one would not stand for.

"Leave him alone." I jumped up off the bed, ready to throttle him. "What are you doing here and when are you leaving?"

"Well, sweetheart, I'm glad to see you're over Suzz's manager Beau and Josh because you've never asked about where they were and if they were okay." He rubbed my arm. "See, I knew we were meant to be together." He tried to wrap his arms around me in a manly hug, but I resorted to my first instinct. I kicked him/her between the legs.

Laughter was not the reaction I was hoping for. Okay, obviously it didn't hurt as much as it would have if Hildy was actually in Gorget form, so I also attempted to pull her hair, not too successfully I admit, but hey, I can take on either a mawl or a femawl. (For clarity, going forward I'll refer to Hildy/Gorget as a femawl and use pronouns, she, her, etc)

Bring it on. I stepped away from her afraid I actually might kill her and she was so not worth going to jail for. Ha! I would prove our little soothsayer wrong.

"Over my dead body," Rotsen jostled himself off the bed and came between us. "You better not have hurt either Josh or Beau."

"And if I did, what would you a *weed* do about it?" Hildy/Gorget hissed. I so did not like her when she turned like that. She was showing her true colors and I didn't like to see them.

"Why you little…" Rotsen lunged, ready to punch the living daylights out of the mouthpiece. Gorget/Hildy in true coward fashion held up his hands.

"I didn't come here to fight; I was trying to help you." She pinched my cheek and then held up her two fingers in a peace sign. "I honestly don't know what happened to Josh or Kaj for that matter."

"I'm working on getting us home and you are so not coming with us." There, that would fix her.

Before I could thump her once again, not that I was a violent person or anything, a knock sounded at the door. "April, it's me Jocko, I need to come in."

Geez at this rate, I'd have more traffic in my bedroom than a major highway.

Chapter 6

"What are you doing in here?" Jocko asked no doubt surprised Hildy was in my room. It wasn't like we were friends or anything. No matter what shape or form she took and especially now I knew she was Gorget.

"I was just checking to make sure she was okay," Hildy said confidently. "I wanted to ensure she took my tea reading in the right way. It is after all for entertainment purposes only and not to be used to actually predict events."

Gawd, she sounded like an infomercial. Thank goodness on Zorca-twenty-three, we can bleep out the ads so we're not subjected to the monotonous and annoying repetition. Though I have to say, I was impressed by the Shaw How guy. He's a pretty awesome fellow. Who knew so many words rhymed with orange?

"Could you please leave us alone? I'd like to have a word with April, if you don't mind?"

Jocko took Hildy/Gorget's arm and non-too gently pushed her toward the door. Funny enough, I wasn't afraid of being alone in the room with Jocko. He might have a permanent scowl on his face, but his attitude was one I was used to, one I could live with. Heck, when you grew up with a dandelion who copped more attitude than any living mawl, you tended to not sweat the small stuff.

When we were alone, he paced in front of the fireplace, back and forth, forth and back. I got dizzy just watching him, not to mention I was afraid he might wear a hole in the carpet, but then again with his moola, I'm sure he could buy a new one.

"Is there something you want to talk about?" I had to break the ice so to speak, even though there wasn't any ice in the room. "I want to go sightseeing." I glanced out the window, relieved to see it was still daylight. With the events of the day, I wouldn't have been surprised to see it was nightfall.

"Yes, there is and it's not easy to talk about." Jocko flicked open and closed the lids on the boxes on the mantel. At least he'd stopped pacing, but I have to admit this clicking noise was even more annoying.

"Come on, you can tell me anything," I said, copping a Dr. Shell tone. I was a huge fan and I could listen with the best of them. Though I have to say it really bugs me, (and yes this is coming from a praying mantis in my original form) that you get involved in the story, and then it's like, "well, if I arrange for the right people to talk to you, can you and will you meet with them?" I don't know about you, but I like closure at the end of an hour (with commercials).

"Well, it's not easy to say…"

Oh gosh, he was going to tell me he had feelings for me. I must elude an animal magnetism towards Earth mawls. I'm going to have to declare myself a deadly weapon or at the very least I could perhaps bottle my scent and sell it alongside L-Loo's latest perfume.

I rearranged myself amongst the cushions trying to

look as flattering as possible. I would have to be kind when I let him down. Easy! I would do it easy. Every girl who wasn't pining for Freaky Freddie had the hots for Jocko, but I wasn't one of them. Okay, the accent was kind of cool. I mean, who wouldn't like to be chatted up by the accent. Imagine how cool their jails must sound. And no, I didn't want to find out for real. It was purely a rhetorical statement.

But to be honest, I wasn't into tattoos. I know they mean a lot to a lot of people, but really when one's whole arm is decorated, and I use the term loosely with 'artwork' it kind of loses its meaning. As they say, everything in moderation.

I decided to make it easy for him, to take a bold step and come right out with it.

Unfortunately, at the same time he spoke.

"What did you say?"

"No, what did you say?" I asked, flabbergasted.

"I said, you have to leave, right now! Immediately! Pack your bags and vamoose!"

"You want me to leave?" I repeated, unsure if I heard him correctly. Why would he want me to leave? I thought he was in love with me. Oh right, that's probably why. He didn't want to ruin his reputation, or no wait, he's probably worried about mine. It's not proper to have a femawl living with a mawl and he was so sweet to worry about me.

"Yes, you have to go." He snapped the final box closed, slamming it shut. "You know how superstitious I am. Well, I've been thinking about Hildy reading the tea leaves and I can't have any bad luck on the tour with us."

"Listen, you don't have to make excuses. I beat

Freaky Freddie fair and square. I can't help it if he's a poor loser." I huffed and puffed like a dragon. In fact, I could almost feel the steam coming out of my ears, I was so mad.

"This has nothing to do with Freaky Freddie. He actually wants you to stay, so you can have a rematch, but I told him no." Jocko leaned against the door frame.

"You're going to throw me out onto the cobblestone street, with only the clothes on my back because of what some two-bit psychic predicted?" I admit I was mad, and not to mention a little shell shocked. I knew from reading the tabloids, movie stars were a little eccentric, okay, some more than a little but this was totally unacceptable.

"No, I'm not."

Relieved, I realized it was all a great misunderstanding and we'd all laugh about it one day, but right now I wanted him out of my room and I needed some peace and quiet.

"I've arranged for you, and I'm assuming Ralb would want to go with you, to stay with my friend David. He's a great bloke and he's willing to let you stay with him until you can find more permanent living quarters." He tossed a lined piece of paper on the bed.

I reached across the vast covering and without thinking ripped the paper in half. "I don't need your tea or symphony. So that's it then." I tried to jump up off the bed, but I became tangled in the sheets and I stumbled out, catching my foot and falling on my side. Stars alive did it ever hurt. Jocko grabbed my arm to help me up and being the femawl I was, I yanked it out.

"Thanks, but I don't need your help."

"So, you don't want to stay with David?" he asked

as he neared the door.

I wasn't stupid. I was in a foreign country where people spoke English but used words I'd never heard before. I would use this David to get my feet on the ground, and then I'd toss him aside and show Freaky Freddie, Jocko, and Hildy what I was made of.

Dang it, if I could get us home, which I planned to do, I could surely survive on the streets of London.

"Don't be silly. David is a great bloke; he'll help you out." He looked uncomfortable, but not embarrassed enough to let me stay. He reached into the front pocket of his jeans and pulled out a whack of money. "I can't leave you stranded here." He tossed the money on the bed, like I was a two-bit, well never mind, you're too young to know what it reminded me of, and opened the door to the room.

"You can take your money and shove it where the sun doesn't shine, which in this bloody country could be just about anywhere." I threw the money back at him.

"I'd appreciate it as well if you didn't go to the tabloids about this." With one hand on the doorknob, he stopped again. "I wouldn't want it to get out how superstitious I am."

"Oh, don't worry, your secret's safe with me." Yeah, right. I didn't owe him any loyalty. He could keep his tree pot ceiling and his private plane. I was a Teenage ALIEN. I could survive on my own, or rather Ralb and I could.

He pulled the door shut after he left and Rotsen scuttled out from between the pillows. "We're so going to fix Gorget."

"Got it in one, my friend, got it in one."

Chapter 7

Every eye was on me as I walked past the kitchen to the front door. It was so quiet in there; you could hear a safety pin open. I didn't need them, I had Rotsen and Ralb. Together we aliens could survive anything you stupid Earthlings could throw at us.

Suzz entered the room, gnawing on a sausage and must have sensed the drama. "Oh, this looks way too intense for me."

"Ralb, are you coming?" I stuck my head into the open doorway and searched out my brother.

He glanced around at Freaky Freddie, Jocko, and Hildy before fiddling with a paper napkin, ripping it into strips. "I've decided to stay."

"What?" *You two-bit traitor. You louse. You major league jerk*. Okay, not only was Gorget not coming with me (I so didn't want him), neither was Ralb. They could both find their own bloody way back to our frigging planet.

"I'm going to stay here—with them." Ralb moved closer to Jocko as if afraid I was going to thump him.

Did I call him a major league coward yet?

"Fine. Glad to see you think water is thicker than blood."

"Do you want some company?" Hildy asked, turning from the Aga where she was making tea. Is that all she did? "I mean, it was kind of my fault you're in this situation."

"Kind of? *Kind of?* You're just a dime-a-dozen tea leaf reader who can't find your way out of a frigging paper bag. Personally, I would rather take my chances on the streets of London alone, than have you with me," I hissed. "If I never see you again it will be too soon."

"Whoa," Jocko said. "Calm down. You're off on a rant and besides, we don't need to resort to name-calling. We're all adults here." He took a sip of tea and flipped open the newspaper. "Keep good karma flowing."

I'll good karma him in a minute. I stomped out through the hallway, took a look in the mirror, and was proud of what I saw. I tucked my hair behind my ears, shoved my shoulders back, and with my *hanaglug* slung over my back, I opened and slammed the door shut when I heard the sound of breaking glass.

The landing where I stood swayed a fraction of a millimeter and I grabbed the wall, so I didn't topple over. My stomach felt a tad queasy, and I swallowed, before pushing myself off from the wall and taking a deep breath.

Cautiously I opened the door and saw the black-and-white tiled floor covered with broken glass.

"Oh, Jocko, come and see what happened. I believe the one who owns the mirror is the one who gets the seven years bad luck." Freaky Freddie whispered.

"Never tick off a femawl." I calmly said, gently closing the door.

Chapter 8

I stomped down the steps, yes, all one hundred and one steps, stopping at each landing and pounding on each of the doors. I'm not proud to say it but I bad mouthed Jocko at every landing.

When I finally got to the street, I slammed the door and sank down on the cobblestone steps. What was I going to do? Where was I going? I had no idea. I was alone, save for a dandelion, in a strange country with no friends, or family I could call on.

Rotsen poked his head out of my *hanaglug* and patted me on the shoulder. "Don't worry, Oas, we've been in worse predicaments and we've always come through."

"I know, but I thought for once, it seemed like we were going to be able to relax and enjoy our trip without having to save the world."

"You should have known better than that." He grinned. "Come on, let's go and meet David. Do you know how to get there?"

"Just a sec." I dug into my pocket and pulled out the ripped pieces of paper Rotsen had gathered up. "It says to get on the Black Line and get off at Archway. Then walk three blocks north and you'll find Holloway Road. Keep walking and eventually you'll get to Annesley Walk and David's at seventy-six." I stopped and leaned against the wall. "Are you sure we should go there? I really don't want anything from Jocko."

"I can understand your dilemma. Whatever you want to do is fine by me." Rotsen wrapped himself around my arm like a living armband. "So, what do you think?"

"I guess we don't want to look a gift horse in the mouth." I really don't get the sayings of the British.

"Now, where do you think we find the black line?" Rotsen asked, relief flooding his voice. "The color in the middle of the road is yellow, not black."

A teenager with pierced eyebrows, lips, and a ring through her nose stopped short in front of us. "Theblacklineisthetube."

"Sorry, did you say something?" I asked, watching the ring in her lip move up and down like a musical instrument.

"Theblacklineisthetube," she repeated.

"I'm sorry, I still don't know what you said."

"Come…with…me!" She spoke so slowly, I'm sure she thought I was clueless, but in my defense, her accent was very thick.

I shrugged and staggered to a standing position. I had nothing to lose. If it didn't work out, I'd just come back here and start from square one or two.

This was one daring femawl. She walked across the two-lane streets without waiting for the friendly hand signs to say she could. Not to make fun of people who weren't as fortunate as I am, but I think she was color blind as well. Even I know red means stop and green means go. But in her colorless world, it all must have blended together because she ignored all of them and treated each the same. When car drivers honked at her, she raised her middle finger in the form of a British wave and continued on her way.

We reached a black opening where three men stood outside the stream of people handing out newspapers. I took one, just to be polite, and reached in my pocket to give him some money. My new-found friend yanked at my arm and hissed in my ear. "They're free."

What a great country this is! You give away free stuff and you have really nice people. I'm not counting those people from Peach Acid in that equation. They were originally from Scotland and while I'm sure there's some nice people in Scotland, they did wear skirts (the men included), played pipes with bags attached (which I personally like the sound of), and had a 'monster' in a lake which to this day hasn't been found. I have my own thoughts on that one, mainly which was it was one smart monster."

She threw some coins in through a little window where a woman sat like a dog in the cage. She seemed happy enough though because she slid tiny pieces of paper back to us.

My friend then held them over a machine which reminded me of a torture device with metal bars moving in rotation. I didn't want to be a wimp with my jaywalking, finger tooting friend, so I bit my lip and followed her through the bars of death.

Oh heavens! I jumped onto the moving steps and began the descent. Gripping the black bar alongside, I held on for dear life, though I was the only one, even an older lady was chatting on her cell phone and not holding onto the moving railing. I've never seen so many moving steps in my life. I tried to keep my mind off the fact I was heading into the bowels of your planet by reading the posters on the side, set at an angle to make reading easy as you descend. Michael Crater, the famous actor who was currently in a play called 'Olive,' was on every other poster. The play 'Fiendish' seemed to be very popular as well as a salute to Pugsby Mantle who many thought was an alien, but we didn't want any credit for that one.

I followed my friend as she crossed the platform and again we stepped onto another set of moving steps and headed even further down. I remember reading in my *mist book* that during WWII, people used to hide in the tunnels when they were being bombed by the "not nice people." I felt a little claustrophobic, so I really didn't relish or ketchup being down here for long. Also, I wasn't a big fan of rats, especially after you-know-who was a rat in Kaj's cage. I think rats hang out down here, so hopefully I wouldn't see any red eyes glaring at me in the dark or my new friend might see a side of me I didn't want her to.

I must have walked on too many of those downwards moving steps because while I waited on the platform, again I felt a slight movement underneath my feet, a faint swaying in the tunnel.

"Crikey, looks like another earthquake," the girl admitted, seemingly unconcerned we were in the bowels of Earth.

"Shouldn't they shut down the trains?" I glanced down towards the tracks, seeing red eyes flash back at me.

"Nah, nothing stops the British trains." She shrugged her shoulders like I was a major wimp and no sooner were the words out of her mouth, it arrived.

With the swoosh of hot air and a strong smell of fuel, an underground train came to a stop, the doors opening right in front of me as I struggled with my earth suitcase. I admit I was extremely uncoordinated when I tried to get me and it in before the doors slammed shut. With a sigh I'm sure Ralb could hear back at the apartment, my friend pulled the case in and rolled it to the back of the train.

"Sit there," she ordered, as she took a seat on the other side of the car. I think it was totally unnecessary; there were lots of empty seats beside and closer to me, but whatev. She obviously knew best.

Every two minutes or so, we'd stop, and more people got on. Pretty soon, it was standing room only. I went to stand up to give a pregnant woman my seat, but the glare from my friend—I so would have to learn her name—kept me seated, but I did scootch over and make room for her.

She got up at the next stop, Tufnell Park, and I followed suit.

"I'm getting off here, but you stay on till Archway." As if to take pity on me, as much as someone with a piercing in her tongue could, she continued. "Let me see the pieces of paper again."

I showed her and she laughed. "Sounds like you're staying with David. You two should get along great." She chuckled again. "At the next stop, just go up the stairs, turn left when you get to the street. I know a shortcut. Go down Holloway until you see an alley. Cut through it and you'll come right up on Annesley Walk."

"How do you know David?" I asked, impressed at what a small world we lived in, ignoring the fact I'd be darting down dark alleys in a foreign country.

"Everyone who lives in this part of the country knows David, but I knew him especially well." She flicked her jet-black hair over her shoulder. "I was married to him for fourteen years."

I don't know what shocked me more. The fact she was old enough to marry to begin with or the fact she had been married for such a long time. She looked like she was still in high school.

I felt a panic attack coming on and I began to hyperventilate. I needed a bag to breathe into or something. I tucked my mouth into my shirt and began to steady my breathing, somewhat.

"Don't worry, you'll find David a real experience." She patted me on the shoulder, much in the fashion Rotsen had done. "Enjoy England and tell David, Betty says hello."

"Thanks for your help and I'll say hi to David for you." Sadly, I watched my only English friend leave the car without a backward glance. Betty! What a common name—no offense intended for the Bettys who might be reading this—for such an uncommon person.

Taking a deep breath, I reminded myself I had to be strong for both Rotsen and myself. I was femawl, I could do it.

Look out, David, whoever you are, you're about to meet your alien match.

Chapter 9

Okay, it really wasn't my fault. I know I'm the only one around save for Rotsen and he really can't be blamed because he's a dandelion and all, but well, here's what happened.

I glanced down at the "free" newspaper that Betty had left on the seat beside me and started reading it.

Rotsen popped his head around my arm, hidden by the newspaper; he wanted me to flip the page to the soap summaries. "Come on, Oas, let me see what's happening next week? Chances are we will be here then."

"What? Don't tell me you don't have faith in me either?" I rustled the paper until I got to the right page. "Fine, read away." While he did, I amused myself with the crossword, I so wasn't going to get into reading the horoscopes on the same page. I've had enough of the stars and their un-alignment.

"You can turn the page, I'm finished reading." Rotsen yawned. "What a great newspaper! I'm all caught up."

"Great," I answered absentmindedly. How wonderful my dandelion is all caught up with his soaps. All is right with the world. You know what they say, happy dandelion, happy life.

"Umm, Oas, did you happen to glance at the last page?" Rotsen asked, caution dripping from every word.

"I really don't care what's going on with your stupid soap." Curiosity got the best of me and I flipped to the last page. "Oh, Heavens."

There in three-inch bold letters stated the words I longed to hear.

CLEAR SKIES AT ROCKHEDGE CIRCLE FOR SUMMER SOLSTICE.

"Hot dog, Rotsen, we're heading to Rockhedge Circle."

"Umm, great idea, Oas, but how are we going to pay for the train ticket?" Rotsen asked. "We don't have any money. Are we going to David's?" Hope filled his voice.

"You bet. We'll throw ourselves on his mercy and then we'll get to Rockhedge Circle and bingo, bango, bongo, we'll be having dinner with my Parental Beings."

I grinned and stretched my arms across the back of the seats. I had the entire car to myself, how cool was that? I love trains. I love the smoothness of the clickity-clack on the line. Okay maybe these don't clickity-clack but they were smooth and I haven't slept in a while and, okay, I frigging admit it, I had a touch of jet leg.

So, sue me, I fell asleep.

It only seemed like seconds later, Rotsen was tickling my ear. I yawned, glanced around me relieved to see we were the only ones in the train car, and wiped a spittle of drool from my chin.

The train steamed to a stop and the doors sucked open. I pushed my way out, past the throng of Brits forcing their way in—man you could tell they weren't

Canadian; Canadians were way too polite.

I stood on the platform and looked at the signs posted in the white tile.

"Covent Garden." I glanced down at Rotsen in horror. "This isn't our stop."

"No kidding, Miss. Explorer."

"Rotsen, we're officially lost."

"Okay, don't panic, remember we're aliens. We can survive on this stupid planet." He always was the voice of reason. His simple words managed to calm me down. "Let's go topside and we'll figure out what to do."

"Good idea." I dragged my suitcase up the moving stairs and out onto the street. I shook my head when a skinny fellow offered me another free newspaper. I've had enough with those frigging free papers.

A couple of teenagers passed me, pushing and shoving and I jumped out of their way. Where were helpful natives when you needed them?

"Love, you look like the type we need." A grey-haired fatherly figure handed me a flyer. He was so tall, I thought at first he was standing on a chair. Man, he could be in the record book. He wore a green plaid jacket with brown patches on the elbows. Just the fact he called me 'love' made me like him. Wow, the thoughts weren't even formed in my head and there was a helpful Brit right there.

"What type is that?" Hesitation filled my voice. I wasn't keen on being sold into slavery, to say the least.

"We need extras for our play, and I think you'd be perfect." He grabbed one of my shoulders and twirled me around like I was a ballerina. Round and round I went until he finally stopped, and I was majorly dizzy.

"Extras for what?" I stumbled over the words. I heard about some of those avant-garde plays where everyone drank wine and removed their clothes.

"Remember we need money for Rockhedge Circle," Rotsen whispered in my ear.

"Is there pay involved?" I asked, getting into it. Rotsen was right. I'd take one for Team Oas, if it meant money.

"Can you sing?" The man asked, ignoring everyone who was walking by. Even the rain drizzling now didn't seem to bother him, though I guess the Brits weren't afraid of a little rain.

"Spend it now,
'cause you can't take it with you.
Buy the Farm and Rent the Cow,
'cause you can't take it with you.
Push the Daisy's from underground
'cause you can't take it with you."

Okay, it wasn't my best effort by far, but the background rain was as good as singing in the shower, though I have to admit I think I did a great job. People stopped and stood three deep, gathering around me in a semi-circle like I was a busker.

"Fantastic," The grey-haired man chimed. "Go through those doors right there and tell them Bramwell sent you."

I did as I was told, parting through the sea of people like I was a celebrity. Brits reached out to touch me and when I finally got to the doors, I barely had the strength to pull it open.

"Well, you certainly pulled a fast one there," Rotsen smirked.

"All in the name of getting home, Rotsen. All in

the name of getting home."

Chapter 10

I blinked several times as I entered the darkness of the theatre. The smell of old plush seats filled my nose as did lemons probably used to polish the gleaming wood. With extreme caution, as if I was a blind femawl, I walked down the slight ramp towards the wooden stage at the front.

"Extras, extras. I need all the extras here now!" A heavy-set man bellowed, his stomach overhanging and trying to escape from his pants. A red beret sat on the top of his grey-haired head, and gladiator sandals covered hairy feet. "Now!"

I joined a row of boys who were shaking in their short pants. The one closest to me must really need the money because his shirt was way too big for him and was torn in stripes. His pants were ripped, and his feet were bare.

"Why haven't you been to wardrobe yet?" The bellowing man shaded his eyes with his hands and glared down at me.

"I just got here," I squeaked out.

"I don't want excuses, just results. We'll just have to go with what you're wearing. I can't believe it. Major amateurs in my play." He flipped his beret off, and then returned it to his head. "Okay, so payday is three weeks from now and it's minimum wage." He held up his hand like he was a traffic cop. "Don't come whining to me about getting more money, or receiving it sooner."

"Oas, did you hear that?" Rotsen snaked his way up towards my ear. "We can't wait that long."

"I know but what am I going to do?"

"Okay, you there. Out! I don't care if you have the voice of an angel, I won't have insubordination in my area," he shrieked.

"Fine, I didn't want to be in your stupid play anyway." I stuck my tongue out at him and walked back the way I came towards the door outside and sane people.

Throngs of folks bustled along the street as I walked down an alley. I sat on an empty soda crate.

"Rotsen, nothing ever works out for me." Even to my own ears my tone sounded defeated. "Maybe I should go back to Jocko and apologize."

"What? Are you frigging kidding me? You really want to see the smirk on Ralb's face when you come crawling back? Suzz will rub it in big time."

"I hadn't thought about that." I sank my head into my hands and tears flowed from my tear *ducks.* "I need money to get us to Rockhedge Circle. How am I going to do it?"

"Well, you were singing pretty good back there," Rotsen whispered so quietly, I wasn't sure I heard him correctly.

"Hey, what about if I sing?" With renewed vigor, I dragged the carton to the main street and climbed up.

"Great idea wished I thought of it," Rotsen replied. "You need something to put the money in."

Right. I glanced around and found a paper coffee cup that someone had left on top of the rubbage can.

Luckily it was an extra-large so I should be GtoG "Okay, Rotsen, here goes nothing."

I cleared my throat of any frogs that might have ventured there and looked up towards the sky for inspiration. I wouldn't give Suzzy and/or Peach Acid the satisfaction of using one of their songs, not that they could hear me or anything. Then it came to me, in a flash, I would sing the song my Parental Being sang to me and her Parental Being to her.

Feebly I began.

"When you wish upon a star,

The star don't care who you are.

The star shines down to give you light

And now your dreams now seem bright

Wonders never cease

Like wrinkles never crease

Dreams are the stuff

To give you hope.

So, wish upon that star tonight and

Your dreams will take flight."

I warbled softly at first, then as I got more confidence my register got higher as did my voice. Coins rained into the cup and I kept singing. It was like the song that never ends. When I finished it, I just vamped up again and away I went. I guardedly glanced down and saw the cup was overflowing. The crowd thickened and I was just about to call it a night when rough hands grabbed me from behind and yanked me off my pedestal.

"Little lady, you don't have a permit to be singing on the street corner. You're under arrest."

Chapter 11

If I had a tin cup, I'd be running it across the bars, but as it was, I was given lukewarm tea in a Styrofoam cup. Teabag out, so basically it was just yucky colored, yucky tasting water. Not something the Brits should be proud of at all.

My cellmates didn't seem to mind it though. I guess it's all what you're used to.

"What you in for, girlie?" A femawl asked, her Porcupine-styled bright colored red hair standing at attention. She cracked her knuckles and flexed her Popeye strong muscles as she waited for my answer.

"Singing," I croaked, the frogs that I thought had vacated my throat had suddenly reappeared forming a colony, actually a group of frogs are called an army, in my windpipe.

"Well, let's hear the little songbird." She punched the wall with a balled fist and turned to face me.

I'd be interested to hear the little songbird as well. I remember when I first arrived my goal was to see a bird and one pooped on my head but didn't sing to me. I waited and waited, but there weren't any songs from any birds.

"She means you." A timid, mousy brunette rubbed her hands together from her seat on the bottom bunk.

"Shut up, Mabel," The first one yelled. "Start singing, sweetheart, or I'll give you something to scream about." She reached over and punched me in the arm.

"Aww." What the heck is she doing? She doesn't have to be mean or anything. How was I supposed to know she meant me?

Quietly at first, then with more vigor I got louder as I got more confident. My other jail mates began to hum along with the chorus as I sang Suzzy's song— "Can't Take it With You."

"Spend it now,
'cause you can't take it with you.
Buy the Farm and Rent the Cow,
'cause you can't take it with you.
Push the Daisy's from underground
'cause you can't take it with you."

I glanced over at Porcupine-head and I admit it I was relieved her eyes were closed and she seemed to be enjoying herself.

I sank down beside Mabel on the wafer-thin mattress, covered with stains I had no interest in determining what they were. I rested my head in my hand and giant sobs racked my body.

What a frigging mess I've made of my Earth life. I was alone—totally and utterly alone. Josh was gone, gone forever. I'd loved and lost the love of my life. I was a girlfriend widow in my teens and I would never love again like I did with him. Definitely a dark cloud was perched over my head since I'd de-planed in this frigging country and not just because it's been raining non-stop.

I missed Josh and something I never thought would happen. I missed Zorca-twenty-three. I missed the arid landscape that made my skin dry out so much I had to use Lizard Lotion and layer it on so thick it was like I had an extra skin. I missed the way the wind wiped around the mountains causing dust bowls so big you could jump inside them. Of course, it goes without saying, I missed my Parental Beings, who were always in my corner even when I wished they were across the room. I have to say, I wasn't in a hurry to meet up again with all my siblings, but you had to take the bad with the good.

Wiping my eyes with the back of my hands, I felt an arm come around my shoulders and I leaned into Mabel, so bone-racky I could almost feel her lungs through her light cotton shirt.

"Don't cry, little lady. It can't be all that bad." She began to hum a tuneless tune. I braced myself in case it rubbed Porcupine-head the wrong way.

"It is," I sniffed. "My boyfriend is gone, and there's no one who's going to bail me out. I'm going to be stuck here forever." I glanced up through reddened eyes and saw that I was the center of attention in the cell. "No offense, intended. If I had to be with anyone, I'm glad it's you guys." I certainly didn't want to get on the wrong side of someone whose hair was considered a deadly weapon.

"You there, there's someone here to see you." A matron used a key on an enormous ring to open the door of the cell.

"Who me?" I pointed to myself and pulled myself up off the mattress, cracking my head on the metal of the overhead bunk bed.

"Come on, I don't have all day." The matron waved her baton like she was leading a parade.

Thank Stars. Somehow Ralb had discovered the

mess I was in and was here to rescue me. Never would I badmouth him again. Never would I call him a name he didn't deserve. Never would I treat him bad. Nope from now on, I would kiss the ground (okay, maybe not that far) he walked on. I gave a little wave to Mabel and slinked out of the cell, following the matron past the other occupied cells and through a long hallway to a booking area.

I glanced around from left to right, over each of my shoulders in search of my brother, but he was nowhere to be seen.

"I really hate to bother you, Ms. Matron, but I think you made a mistake. There's no one here for me." Deflated I sat down on one of the cracked orange plastic chairs.

"Gather your stuff together, you're coming with me."

Chapter 12

I ran to keep up with him, but it was like trying to keep pace with a rushing Giant. I had to skip to hold pace with him, the suitcase which held all my belongings that I'd retrieved from the matron rubbed against my legs.

"Why did you come?" I asked, my breath coming out in fits and bursts. When I got a minute to myself, I really was going to have to sign up for some Yoga classes to get my breathing under control.

"We have a policy of not allowing buskers on our street corner outside the theatre, can't have the competition you know. I'm Bramwell, just Bramwell." He was the one who'd originally handed me the flyer to join his play continued, "I don't know why Michael Crater didn't want you in the play." He shook his head. "Who can understand the way some of these theatrical folks think."

"Wow, I've heard of Michael Crater. In fact, when I was traveling down into the bowels of the subway, I saw his posters all over the walls." I tugged at his arm to get him to slow down. "What's the hurry?"

"I have to get back to work. If Michael sees me gone, he'll have my head." Bramwell raced on.

"Bramwell, could you please stop a minute?" I bent over double in an attempt to catch my breath. Finally, after numerous gasps, I got my breathing under control.

"I'll be out of your hair in no time, but I need money to get to Rockhedge Circle."

"No can do!" Bramwell stopped at the red light and without catching my eye or glancing down towards me, he joined the group of people and strutted across the street when the light changed color.

"But it's mine. Just give me the money I earned before I was thrown in the hoosegow and we'll call it a day."

"No can do," he repeated. "I used the money to pay the fine and get you out. It's spent. There's nothing left. He sharply made a turn to the left and I received an elbow in my forehead for my troubles.

I grabbed his jacket sleeve and pulled him to a stop. "You don't seem to understand. It's a matter of life and death that I get to Rockhedge Circle. You've got to help me. You've got to, please." Tears welled up in my eyes and dripped down onto his jacket sleeve. I couldn't help myself, I used it to wipe away my tears and dry my nose which was suddenly dripping like a melting icicle on a Zorcan-twenty-three summer day.

Rudely he yanked his sleeve away and dug into the left pocket of his faded jeans. "Here. This is all I've got." Golden coins dropped into my hands like the rush of a waterfall. "If you want any more, you're going to have to talk to Michael himself."

"How am I supposed to do that?" I asked. "He doesn't want anything to do with me."

"Hang around the back door of the theatre. You're a smart girl, I'm sure you'll figure something out." Bramwell pulled open the back door of the theatre and thrust himself inside, before slamming the door on me.

I sank down against the aged red brick wall of the

playhouse and stretched my walking sticks out in front of me.

"Is it safe for me to come out now?" Rotsen asked, poking his head out from the pocket of my shirt.

Tugging him out of my pocket, I wrapped him around my wrist, so his face was opposite mine. "So, any ideas?"

"Well, for one thing, you have to step out of this flipping depression that you're in and get with the program," Rotsen reamed me out. He always had a way of cutting to the quick when it came to my moods. "Next thing, you're going to use your Zoran-given talent and get out of this mess."

"Rotsen, if I start singing again, I'm going to be right back in the slammer and frankly I couldn't face any more jail time with Porcupine-head." Geez, I really was going to have to find out her name, but maybe not, since I never had the intention of seeing her again anytime soon.

"For cripes sake, Oas, use your connections. Let's go to David's house and ask him for help. There's nothing to be ashamed of to ask for assistance." Rotsen smirked. "Come on, pull yourself up off those cobblestones and let's get moving."

I leaned over and kissed his slightly bruised head. "What on Earth would I ever do without you?"

"You're never going to have to find out, sweetheart." Rotsen rubbed his leaves against my wrist. "Now, see that old lady over there, the one who looks like a Queen."

I glanced over to where he was pointing and saw an elderly woman, bent over a wooden walking stick. A checkerboard handkerchief covered her head and a brown tweed skirt reached just past her knees.

"Rotsen, she looks as much like the Queen as I do," I said. "What about her?"

"You're going to go over to her and ask her kindly and I mean kindly for enough money to go and visit your sick father," Rotsen ordered. "Then we're going to get on the tube, go to David's and get out to Rockhedge Circle where we're going to walk into the rocks on the summer solstice and get back to Zorca-twenty-three where we'll wake up and realize this was all a bad dream."

"Yes, sir." I dodged a boy with his cap on backward as he careened towards me on his skateboard. In his effort to avoid me, he ran right into the old woman, knocking her over. Her handkerchief hung askew, her skirt ripped, and a shoe bounced down the sidewalk.

"Hey, jerk, can't you even stop to say you're sorry?" I screamed at his retreating back. I really can't believe the youth of today, no respect for the elderly. I know I can't speak for all the youths, I mean, if you're the type reading about my adventures then you for sure aren't the type, I'm grouping in with skater boy.

He turned around, gave me one of those famous one-finger salutes, and grinned. If I wasn't so concerned about the woman, I'd give chase, and hunt him down and well, I don't know what I'd do. Probably push him off his ruddy board, that would certainly fix his apple cart.

"Cheers," the lady spoke in the poshest of British accents, usually reserved for a Queen and her immediate family.

"No worries." Helping her up, I noticed her nylons

were torn. I went to retrieve her shoe. "Let me help you. Lean on me while you get your balance."

"Dearie, you're much too kind. Let me offer you some money for your troubles." She reached into her brown leather purse, one handle now ripped off and hanging dangerously by a thread.

"No really, I don't need any money." Okay, I know you know I did, and I know Rotsen knew I did, but really, I couldn't take money from the old dear. It was probably the only money she has until her next pension check comes in.

"I insist." She forced the folded paper into my hand and then squeezed my hand tight.

"Really, you must take it back. If you could tell me please how to get to Annesley Walk, that's all I'd need from you." I had my pride.

"I can do better than that. Here's my driver now. He'll drive us there." I glanced over to where she was pointing her walking stick to see the shiniest black car I've ever seen. A tall, posh man wearing a driving cap, fingerless leather driving gloves, and a tight black suit jacket, jumped out of the front of the car and held the door open for us. I followed my new best friend into the brown leather confines of the car, the door purring shut behind us.

"I'm Jezebel, and what's your name?" she asked as I took in the surroundings. From the leather console in the middle which she popped open, she removed a bag of ChocoCircles, offered me some before shifting some into her hand and clasping them to her mouth.

"I'm Oas, err April." I barely got the words out before a burst of chocolate hit my taste buds and not any ordinary chocolate either. British chocolate.

Believe me, and this is just my opinion, when I say there's no other better in the world, even the Swiss can't compete, though to be honest, they do make really good yodelers.

"What an unusual name for such an unusual girl." Jezebel laughed as she flipped on the television tucked in the seat in front of us. The theme song from Kono Street filled the car and I knew it was all Rotsen could do not to poke his head out to watch.

"Jezebel isn't all that common either," I said, wishing she'd offer more of the chocolate.

"It is if you're a gypsy."

Chapter 13

"Wow, that must have been cool growing up as a gypsy!" Imagine, not having to go to school, living life as a nomad. I would give my back teeth to have Parental Beings who would be so flexible. I'm sure it's different now but that's what I imagined.

"We were called travelers and it was kind of fun, but not when you're married off at sixteen." Jezebel muted the television while there was a commercial on.

"Sixteen? I can't even find a boy to date, never mind marry." That was just too crazy. I mean, I loved Josh and all, wherever he might be, but I certainly had no intention of marrying him. Geez, I wasn't even sure at this point in time, given the fact he's AWOL and all, that I still even wanted to date him.

"Colin, why don't you drop Oas here at the corner and we'll drop the car around back? Oas, just keep walking up this street, turn left and you'll find David's."

I told Colin I could let myself out and thanked her numerous times for the ride and she insisted on handing me some paper money. Thanking her now for the money, I stepped outside and breathed a sigh of relief before I immediately began to cough. I followed her directions to the letter (what a funny saying that is). Soot filled my nose, ears, and eyes but I staggered onwards. Turning left, I followed the street passing homes all attached, little grass yards at the front. It was amazing what people could fit in such a small space. One had a rusty car, another an orange couch, and two reclining chairs. I guess this part of the town hadn't heard of lawnmowers, because the grass was high and very weedy. Rotsen, if he wasn't such a snob, would have felt very at home there.

This really didn't seem like the type of area that a shiny black car belonged. Maybe it was on loan.

Taking a deep breath, I turned down into the alley and became totally immersed in the artwork. There were no mere graffiti drawings of 'Kat loves Mick' or obscene drawings of mawl and femawl body parts, but rather it was like a garden came to life on the bricks. Ten-foot-high lupines, in an array of flattering colors, neighbored with twelve-foot-high Roman buildings. I would normally be in a hurry to get out of such a confined space, but this time I stopped and lingered. I had to take in all the artwork. The artist was extremely talented. Every time I looked back at the walls, I saw something new, something hidden, in the original paintings. When at first, I noticed the Roman architecture, at second glance I saw little frogs poking their heads around the pillars, small snakes intertwined among the faux marble outcroppings.

Then in a smooth transition, Shakespearean scenes were played out, Juliet in her balcony, the faux painting done so well, I felt like I was indeed in the act myself, as the wood nymphs frolicked about Romeo's feet.

Rotsen shoved his head out, no doubt wondering what the hold-up was.

"Wow!" He voiced my thoughts exactly. He twisted his head around to view the wall behind me.

"Did you see that? I think that picture just moved."

I turned to see what he was watching, and an entirely new vision engulfed my eyes. Instead of the Roman drama unfolding, this wall contained the famous landmark of Rockhedge Circle, robed men and women surrounding the stones, the red orb you call the Sun shining through.

"I think you're imagining things. It didn't move it's the way the artist has laminated the orb, so it seems to be flying directly at the stones and therefore right at us." I was more concerned about what the picture was trying to tell us. "I think it's the summer solstice," I whispered. "That's the time of year when Ralb said we could get home. The rocks shift slightly and with the power from the sun, it's a time machine." Excitement filled every word. "We'll be able to get home."

Always the voice of reality, Rotsen chimed. "Hopefully it comes before we are witness to the death Gorget-slash-Hildy claimed would happen."

"Come on! Let's get settled into David's and we'll get this show on the road."

With a spring in my step, I rushed out of the alley, anxious to get to where we were going. I double-checked the address and stopped in front of seventy-six.

"Wow," Rotsen said. "Okay, is it just me or does it seem like there was a sale on paint and this David took advantage."

"Shh, he might hear you."

"Right, and it would never occur to him that someone might point that out to him." Rotsen sighed. "I don't think I'm telling him something he doesn't already know. Let's hope not, or we're in bigger trouble than even I could have imagined," he said before popping down into my sweatshirt pocket.

The house could only be described as if it were dropped down from the nineteen sixties. Rainbows of color were splashed across the front of the bricks, not in any apparent row or order. Blue bricks sat beside red, beside orange, beside purple, beside yellow. On the next row, the colors fought for attention with neon shades. At least the window shutters were uniform, even if that color was bright red.

The roof was another matter entirely. I would have thought slate roofs would have been a thing of the past, but apparently not in this David's world. Grey, cracked, some missing completely, tiles rubbed against a small open dormer window, where a lace curtain fought to escape.

The garden was a sight to behold. Where the neighboring ones were tip dumps, this one was an urban oasis. A white picket fence surrounded the small enclosure, stone footpaths led off to different garden rooms, one leading to a small Greek statue of some goddess who didn't have arms. Another path led to a love seat made of willow, its bulging cushions, plain beige, and almost a shock to the senses since it was so plain. I saw another path go off towards an arbor, the purple flowers cascading into a beautiful waterfall.

Surrounding the water feature, was a four-foot-by-four-foot square of sand, with nary a footprint, bird marking or any such disturbing the serenity of the area.

I opened the gate, a small bell jingling my arrival and I felt weird dragging my suitcase into this serene garden. Instead, I picked it up and carried it through the arbor towards the front door.

Before I could ring the dragon-shaped doorbell, the

door popped open and I was enveloped in a warm bosom.

"Welcome, my child. We've been awaiting your arrival."

Before I could stop the embrace, the door slammed shut and I was in a darkened house.

What had Jocko gotten me into?

Chapter 14

"Is David here?" I asked as I struggled to breathe. I kept inhaling the scent of jasmine. Her breasts were like gigantic fluffy pillows. My Parental Being was slim, with no cushioning so to feel such an embrace was startling.

"What do you want with David?" she asked, loosening her grip. I took advantage of the opportunity to step back and take a gander at my hostess.

Stars above, she must be hot. Not hot, like good looking, but hot in all the clothes she wore. She had on more layers than an onion. Dressed totally in black, she wore a long skirt, laced up black boots, leather from my uninformed observation, and five sweaters, all too small, lacking coverage of her two assets.

A lace shawl covered her head, and draped down along her shoulders, hiding her face.

"Umm, sorry to bother you, but I was sent to stay with David by a friend of his."

She walked to the light switch and pushed it inwards, releasing a gas-lit glow down the long, pink-flowered wallpapered hallway. Pictures adorned both sides of the wall, some of famous people, but all on black velvet.

As I heard myself, I thought maybe she'd think I was either a free-loader or at the very least someone running from the authorities. I've learned through my *wad,* honest to goodness hardworking folks don't really like to harbor criminals. Not that I was guilty of any new crimes, Bramwell had paid my dues and I'd done my time.

"I intend to pay my way," I reached into my pocket and pulled out the whack of cash that Jezebel had so kindly given me. "How much is it a night?"

She zeroed in on the money like she was a mosquito, and it was fresh flesh.

"That will do." With movements quicker than a gecko's tongue, she pocketed it all.

"Here let's go and have a nice shot of sherry." She started to pull me towards the back of the house when a knock interrupted us.

At the door, a mawl was shading his eyes, peering inside through the small window.

"Just ignore him." She pulled at me again, much like an annoying sibling who wants you to play with her. Believe you me, I've had plenty of experience of that feeling with all my siblings. My Parental Beings figured if they had enough off-spring then they wouldn't have to entertain us. Frankly, I think they could have stopped at four, five, maybe six. Six hundred plus siblings to me seems a tad extreme, don't you agree?

"Jezebel, it's me, David."

"Jezebel?" This couldn't be the same invalid with the walking stick who gave me money and took me for a ride in the shiny black car.

"Yes, my little cumquat. It is me." I noticed Colin framed in the background of the door, holding his driving cap.

"Jezebel, let her go."

Chapter 15

With moves I'd perfected trying to get out of Ralb's clutches when we were younger, I yanked my arm and ran towards the door. Throwing it open, I blinked in the sunlight, and not wanting to wait until my eyes focused, I screamed at the mawl. "Are you the friend of Jocko's?"

Without waiting for his acknowledging nod, I ran out of the house to stand behind him. I had to avoid the clutches of Jezebel or I might get sucked in.

"Jezebel!!" David put his dark sunglasses on the top of his curly brown-haired head. "Didn't we have a chat about you lying to my guests?"

"Aww, come on David. I get so lonely over here with my paintings. I want to visit with real people."

"I'm sure, umm, sorry what's your name?" He waited for me to supply him with the info. Geez, how many house guests did this joker get?

"April…"

"I'm sure April and I can make time to drop over for a visit, in a fortnight."

Jezebel burst into tears, but apparently, they were tears of joy. She used the veil to wipe away the drips. "Really, I would really enjoy that, but please call first. I don't like to be interrupted during my stories." She folded the money I gave her when I thought I was renting a room and tucked it down the front of her top.

"Umm, that's my money," I whispered to David as he led me outside.

"No, it's mine. I gave it to her and now I'm taking it back." Firmly, she shut the door, leaving us on her front step.

"The money is fake. If you looked closely you would have seen her picture on it. Sorry, you had to meet one of my neighbors that way. Believe it or not, she's really a kind person. She looks after my dogs when I'm away and they get so spoiled, they're always trying to sneak out of the house and head across the road to get some of her special treats." He laughed. "I don't know if I want to know what she puts in them or not, but the dogs like it."

"She gave me a ride here, but I don't know how she managed to change clothes so quickly. She dropped me off at the front door and said she was driving around back. I admit though I did spend some time looking at all the wonderful artwork."

"Yes well, her mother was in the circus, so she learned how to change clothes quickly and her father was a gypsy, er, a Traveler and when he died, he left her a fist full of money. She rents fancy cars and Colin's her son who goes along with her," he lowered his voice. "Probably thinks he's going to end up with some of her real money."

"Is she okay? I mean, is she all right in the noggin?" I didn't want to be mean, but I had to know. Maybe they should use some of her money to get her head fixed up.

"Oh, she's harmless. Nice old bird, she is. Never hurt a flea." He tucked his longish brown hair behind both ears and led me down the garden path. No really, he did lead me along some flagstones towards the road.

"So, you don't live here?" I surrendered my suitcase, and he hefted it up with one hand like it was a one-pound weight.

"Nah, I live there—Sixty-seven Annesley Walk. Jocko is always getting the numbers mixed up. I think he's dyslexic, but he won't get himself tested. Good thing I helped him with his homework, or he'd still be working on his A levels."

With all the beautiful artwork by Jezebel's, I hadn't noticed the small, converted church directly across the way.

Uneven stones covered the front where two massive stained-glass windows sided the timber arched door.

"Really! You live here?" I asked in awe. It was just so cute. My enthusiasm got the best of me and I voiced my thoughts. "Come on! I can't wait to see the inside."

Grinning, he held Jezebel's gate open and I rushed across the road. What were his dogs thinking? If I lived here, I'd never want to leave.

"Go ahead. Push the door open."

The black metal knob seemed to be a little stuck, so when I shouldered it, I almost fell on my butt.

"Go easy on the old girl. She was built during the Crusades."

"Really? Next you'll be telling me it was one of the stops for the Knights Templar." Hey, what can I say? I saw all the movies on my *wad* just like everyone else on your planet and I'm pleased to say I read the books as well.

The room was filled with normal everyday furniture and totally inhabitable useable space with a red couch along the far wall, a big screen television set over top of a bricked fireplace, where even today at the end of March, a fire's embers glowed.

A compact kitchen stood to the right of the door, a table and four chairs sat by a patio door overlooking a lush garden.

Five little white faces pushed their noses against the screen and thrilled by the sound of their owner's voice, began to bark in unison.

He followed me inside and put my case on the floor by the door. "Do you like dogs?"

"Love them and even if I didn't, I am a guest in your house, and I'd put up with them. Bring them in, please."

A snowstorm erupted inside the house when he opened the door. They rushed towards David, then towards me. They were so cute I bent down to pet each of them.

"What are their names?" I asked as I stood back up, only to be jumped on again by the littlest one.

"Daisy, Mildred, Catherine, Victoria, and the little one is Pepperpot."

"So, this house survives all these dogs?" I laughed as Pepperpot picked up a tennis ball and dropped it at my feet. "What breed are they?"

"West Highland Terriers and once you've had a Westie, they spoil you for life and you can't have, and you don't want another dog." He smiled proudly. "I got all of them from the shelter."

"Aww, that's why there's no theme to the names." I stroked the downy fur and scratched behind their ears. To be honest, I've never seen a canine in person before, but I know I liked to be stroked behind my antennas, so

I thought I'd give it a try.

"So how long have you lived here?" I asked as I sat down on the red sofa and was immediately surrounded by each of the dogs vying for my attention. I could get used to this.

"My grandfather gave it to me when I was in my twenties. I was still in Uni at the time, so it sat empty for a year. That's why I'm grateful to Jezebel, she really kept an eye on things for me."

"I'm sure she doesn't miss much that goes on in the street." I laughed as Pepperpot nudged my hand.

"That's for sure. Anyway, when I got my degree, I decided I'd be stupid to live anywhere else, so I got a job locally and here I am."

"This house is really awesome, but you didn't answer my question about the Knights Templar." I smiled. "Everything in England is old, can you imagine if the walls could talk?"

"Well, I don't know about that, but I've had that corner rock radiocarbon dated and, oh never mind, it's probably a lot of hooey," he said modestly.

"Come on, you have to tell me," I pleaded. I tried to think of something really horrid to do. "I'll wash up after dinner if you tell me." Okay, what do you really think of me? Did you really think I'd do something terrible to David if he didn't tell me? The mawl just saved me from who knows what at the hands of Jezebel. I wasn't about to tick him off. Plus, he might take these dogs away from me. I was falling in love already. *With the dogs. Geez*!

"Well, that's an offer I can't pass up." He laughed. "Besides, I was going to tell you anyway." He walked across the room, bypassing the one piece of furniture which looked like it belonged in an old castle, a small table, to the white stone, holding up the corner of the building. "When I had the stone dated…" He held up a framed document from the table beside and handed it to me. "Could you read it out loud? I still get goose bumps hearing it."

The document was from Dr. Charles Leveare B.Sc, M.D. D.A.S, of the Aberdeen University in Aberdeen, Scotland.

"This document confirms on July twenty-sixth, nineteen hundred and ninety-seven, a piece of rock was removed by Professor Charles Leveare of the University of Aberdeen for the purpose of radiocarbon dating. Scrapings taken from the stone located at the above address, determined it to be a bluestone. Further testing revealed antler markings. It is widely known such tools were used as picks. E type and time period from that of Rockhedge Circle, dating to approximately 2500 BC. The same stone, from the same time period as that at Rockhedge Circle and Avebury." The paper was signed, Prof Charles Leveare.

Stunned, I almost dropped the paper. "Are you kidding me?"

Chapter 16

"No, I'm not, and not to brag too much, there's really two stones." He smiled and led the way over to the corner. "They are so tight together, that the sun has to hit them just right to show the crack between the two."

"Let me guess, it happens twice a year." I hardly could contain my excitement. To think such a piece of history was here and I was standing so close to it. I jumped up off the couch, startling Pepperpot who was almost asleep in my lap. Walking across the room, I was pulled by a strong vibration. I reached out and touched them, and the energy that reverberated through me— *Ouch*! A strange and yet strong electric shock ripped through my body, almost throwing me off my feet. I grabbed onto David for support and he managed to steady me somewhat, though my force tilted him a little off center as well. I put one hand on the table, and it seemed to ground me more than anything else. I ran my fingers across the strange markings, vibrations reiterating through each caress:

" When the sun day
reaches its peak
you shall find
what you so
seek"

"Wow, what was that?" He steadied me onto my

feet and ensured I was okay before letting go. "I've never seen the stones affect anyone in that way before." He touched the rocks himself, like one would touch a piece of wood for good luck. "I didn't feel anything." His eyes downcast, he continued. "To answer your question, yes, twice a year, the sun shines through the stones causing a straight cut line right through the room, up the wall, and ending at that window."

He pointed towards the smaller of the stained-glass window to the left of the doorway. Unlike the other windows, each of which were arched, the colored glass of each depicting a rose, this one was different, in fact, slightly odd and misplaced.

Instead of an arch-shape, it was in the shape of an octagon. Twelve diamond shapes contained letters. As if drawn by an unseen force, I walked toward the window to get a closer view.

Letters jumbled into the words—Stones al one!

"What's the story about the window?" I asked totally intrigued with the markings. "It's so unusual."

"I wish I could tell you." He headed towards the kitchen. "How about a cuppa tea?"

"Sounds great." I was surprised and wondered why he was so anxious to talk about the stones, but not so much the window. "So, tell me about your grandfather?"

"He was a character and, if you will, he was even more eccentric than Jezebel. In fact, rumor had it those two were an item at one time." He laughed and I have to admit I liked the sound. It reminded me of a wind chime, but not one of the cheap ones which sound really tinny, but the lovely musical ones.

"No way! I can't imagine Jezebel with anyone." I

smiled.

"I know, I thought that myself, but later I'll show you a picture in the library of the two of them together." At that point, the kettle whistled, and he set about making the tea. "Would you rather have coffee? I have both."

"As long as you promise not to read my leaves, I'll have tea." I shuddered at the memory of Gorget/Hildy's revolution.

"Hey, everything happens for a reason and I for one am not as superstitious as Jocko." He poured boiling water into the teapot where he'd previously placed two teabags and with the hands of an expert, put a little knitted sweater over the pot. The smell of strawberries filled the air, even from the distance. "I remember him from school. I was older, of course. He had to wear the same shirt five days in a row." He set about getting cups out of the cupboard and set them on the table. "Not that his family couldn't afford clothes for him, but he had to wear it without spilling anything on it." He poured out the tea, obviously unsatisfied with the color because he removed the lid and poured the little bit back into the pot. "We had a lot of fun with him."

He sang the famous lyrics:
"Spend it now,
'cause you can't take it with you.
Buy the Farm and Rent the Cow,
'cause you can't take it with you.
Push the Daisy's from underground
'cause you can't take it with you."

His deep voice gave a different dimension to the words than when Hildy and Suzz sang it and not that I was dishing them or anything, but to my ears it sounded better, much better.

"How did he get so famous?"

"Have you been living under a rock?" He didn't know how close he was to the truth with that statement.

"I don't read the tabloids much."

"Good, girl, I too find them to be trash, even when I know the people they're writing about." Again he poured out the tea. This time, the liquid made it into the two cups. "He was always into music. Freaky Freddie, believe it or not, is the brains behind Peach Acid, the driving force, so to speak."

"Really, he didn't seem too forceful when he was almost naked on the plane." I sipped the tea and found it to be perfect. Few people can truly make a great cup of tea, but David was obviously one of a dying breed. I wondered if his grandfather taught him.

"What?" He spit his tea across the room, laughing. "I didn't hear anything about that. Oh gawd, you have to tell me. I'd so love to have one up on smug Freaky Freddie."

"There's not really much to tell. He invited me to play Strip Poker."

"What a rascal!"

"Well, the joke was on him, because it turned out I was quite good at the game, and him, well, not so much." I smiled remembering his embarrassment. Yes, David was right. It was good to put him in his place.

"Remind me never to get involved with you playing cards." He reached around behind him, pulled open the middle drawer, and withdrew a package of chocolate cookies. "Sorry, I should have got these out at the same time. Usually, my partner Michael is here to help out."

"So what business are you and Michael in? You never said." I felt comfortable enough in his company to help myself to more of the delicious tea.

"What is she doing here?" A mammoth mawl pushed open the door and the dogs who up until now had been sleeping contently at my feet jumped to attention and slid across the floor, their toenails scraping along the tiles. With the hands of a surgeon, he managed to pick up all five of the dogs and came into the kitchen. David popped up out of his chair, pulled one out for the guest, and retrieved another cup from the cupboard. "Are you stalking me?"

Flabbergasted, my mouth flew open, and unfortunately the tea I had it in sprayed across the table. The man from the theatre was standing in the kitchen.

"She's April, sent over from Jocko's." David poured tea, brought a china plate to the table, and emptied the package of cookies, up until now in their store-bought packaging, before sitting down again. "What's up?"

He shifted a dog onto his lap, freeing up a hand, and extended it to me. "This girl auditioned for me today, then left without a word."

"I'm sorry, sir." I was ready to eat any kind of humble pie that was going around, just so I could stay in this cozy house. "I needed money sooner than the paycheck you were offering." I wasn't about to tell him he scared the bejeezus out of me. Obviously, he forgot his rant against me talking during his lesson. I thought I'd try the suck up route.

"I can't believe I'm sitting and having tea with Michael Crater, the famous Shakespearian actor." I looked from one to the other. I squealed like a teenage girl. "I saw you in that play. Your last soliloquy still gives me goose bumps."

"I think you have a fan." David laughed.

"Nice to know there's one out there." He smiled shyly. "Even in England, Shakespeare isn't as popular as say 'Fiendish.'"

"I saw the poster for that on the tube." I even impressed myself with my English lingo. "But really who wants to go and see a yellow witch when they can see history being made. I mean," I rushed the words out. "You are saying the words written by William Shakespeare, a true genius." Looking around the room. "He might have ventured into this church to get inspired or repent his sins."

"I like the way this girl thinks." The two men laughed.

Of course, not knowing when to keep my trap shut, I continued. "So how are you two partners if you're an actor, Michael." Look at me, I was on a first name basis with Michael Crater. "I don't remember seeing you in the play."

"I work behind the scenes. I painted the sets."

"And very well I might say. He's the one who brought the play to life." He stroked David's arm. "I don't know if you've seen the alley or not, but David did the artwork in it."

"I did."

"April, David is my husband."

Chapter 17

"No, he can't be because Betty told me she was married to you." I stumbled on. "Betty took pity on me on the street and led me here. She showed me the map on the tube, told me where to get off, and said she was married to you." I paused. "I'm not making it up, she did say she was married to you."

"And she was."

Open mouth, insert size ten feet. I could feel my face redden. "I'm sorry. I'll leave. It's really none of my business and I'll go. Maybe Jezebel has some room." I jumped up, again startling the dogs. Pepperpot even gave me an evil glare, before settling back down at my feet.

"Don't be silly. If you sit down, we'll try to explain." Michael ran a hand through his grey-white hair, tucking the straight locks behind his left ear, where a small diamond sparkled. "Many years ago, more than I'd care to remember, I was in a popular soap opera. 'Chalk Farm' was 'the' most talked about show on television."

He seemed lost in his memories, and it took a couple of minutes for him to continue. "It was the first reality show of its kind, not like nowadays where young men actually have a harem before they pick a mate. 'Chalk Farm' told the tale of my family, the ups and downs of running a farm, then taking the produce to market."

He smiled and continued. "I know, by today's standards it's a little boring, and there's only so much you can do to jazz up and make an exciting farm life. The money they paid was fantastic, though, and helped to pay off our farm debt. We could see the money trough drying up, so as a last-ditch effort, I was forcibly asked by my father to become a dating mongrel. I was photographed with models, leaving restaurants and bars with a different girl every night."

David jumped in. "The headlines they came up with were really creative."

"Don't bring out the scrapbook," Michael warned but like a lightning bolt, David was up and back from the table with a large photo album which he placed in front of me.

Pepperpot climbed into my lap and I shifted her so I could see the book.

A younger Michael was on the cover of You Got It magazine, with Christy Briiony, the headline screaming "Chalk UP Another One," the next page with a Princess, "Royally Chalked Up." There must have been fifty pictures of him with various British stars from different newspapers, tabloids, and magazines. I recognized a young Johnjohn Birch before he became a Sir, each of the Spruce Girls in various poses and one with a smiling Vickee Gengham. Yes, I had to look twice at that one as well.

"Are you finished?" Michael gently closed the book and picked up his story. "Anyway, it was all for show, of course, I had never had feelings for any female in my life. They were great to watch and study to get fashion tips, but as far as romantic feelings, never."

"I could see where that might be a problem." I stroked Pepperpot's ears, and I swear she moaned when I scratched behind her large ears.

"You got it in one. There's only been one person for me my entire life and he's sitting right here." He reached out and ruffled David's hair. "The tabloids were happy with all the publicity, the station was happy, everyone was happy."

"Except Even Childs."

"Except Even Childs," Michael repeated David's statement. He sighed before continuing. "Even Childs worked for Tabloid of the World."

"That rag," I knew it wasn't really a rag, but it was the type of newspaper where they wrote about fat aliens and their anal probes. I mean, knowing me as you do, do you really think we'd travel through black holes just to investigate someone's body parts? Even the Edoricks who landed by default at Area Fifty-one weren't into probing. They were into eating, and when I saw the inside of one once on Zorca-twenty-three, I was astonished. It was like a walking garbage dump.

"Right!" Michael confirmed. "Even Childs went to the same school as I did and he was always on the outside looking in."

Confusion passed across my face. "Why didn't you let him in?"

"I mean, he wasn't popular and while I might not be the most popular kid at school, I did have my core set of friends, some of them were popular."

"Okay." I felt comfort in the company of these two men, as well as the dogs. Funny, how I felt at home here when I was actually a gazillion miles away from home.

"So, fast-forward and I'm on Chalk Farm and he's a quote reporter unquote."

"He was gunning for you," I said, surprising myself with the terms.

"You're right. While he didn't know for sure about me—I did keep a pretty tight lid on it in those days—he had his suspicions."

"What a jerk!"

"So Even became like a second skin to me, tailing me till all hours of the day and night. One night, just after I'd won an American award called an Asocar, I had to do a video acceptance speech. Life was good, I was in love for the first time in my life, and I wanted to share it. I thought I was very covert. A spy would have been proud of my maneuvers. I switched cars, switched clothes, and switched hair pieces."

"It was quite a night," David confirmed, smiling. "Then Even ruined it."

"He took a picture of me leaving David's house in the early morning, with a huge smile on my face."

"That doesn't sound too incriminating," I replied as Pepperpot sighed contently.

"No, and it wasn't, but I didn't know he also had a telephoto lens which he used to photograph inside the house and he got some footage which he shouldn't have."

"And so to shut down Even's photo's I married Betty," David chirped in. "With me in a 'normal' relationship, he lost his ammunition."

"How is Betty?" Michael asked. "We haven't seen her in weeks."

"I was shocked she was old enough to marry," I admitted. "She doesn't look old enough to drive on the roads, never mind old enough to drink at her own wedding."

"She's got good genes."

"Well, she was a good sport for going along with it."

"She's my sister," David laughed. "And she got paid very well."

Michael flipped his hair over his collar and poured more tea into his cup, the previous light brown-colored liquid now a dark black. "And that sums up our sorry little life. Now, tell us all about you."

Chapter 18

Stars above, I hated it when people asked me that. How can I answer without appearing I belong in the loony bin? I couldn't tell them the truth, even if they had come clean with their secrets. There was only one Earth mawl who knew my secret alien lifestyle and I hadn't seen Josh since we'd landed in New Zealand.

"Well, you know Jocko and his superstitions." I hoped one of them would jump in with a Jocko superstition story, but the only noise in the room was when Daisy jumped down off Michael's lap and began to lap water from the bowl. "I knew Suzzy from Bedrocktown and came along for the ride." Well, it wasn't a lie. I just didn't divulge all the extra details of the adventure.

"You must be tired." David glanced over at Michael. "She met Jezebel today," he said as way of explanation. "Why don't I show you your room and you can have a lie down? I'll call you when dinner's ready."

"Why not give her the paper to read? She can catch up on the daily happenings," Michael teased. "Nothing ever goes on in our neck of the woods, so it should put you to sleep no problem."

"Thanks, that would be great." Now that he mentioned it, I was exhausted. I followed him across the small hallway to a door at the right of the front door that I hadn't noticed. He opened it and inside was an antique wooden dresser, brass knobs gleaming in the daylight. A brass bed, the headboard an intricate design of flowers and leaves, showcased fluffy yellow pillows and a flowered comforter.

"Make yourself at home and I'll come and get you when dinner's ready."

"Thanks." The door was almost closed, when a little black nose poked itself into the opening, followed by Pepperpot who jumped up on the bed, turned around in three circles, then curled up into a circle on the bed. "Glad to see you're comfy."

Rotsen poked his head out of my pocket and grunted. "Not even a bit of cookie could you throw my way! Not even a crumb could make it into my tiny jaws." Dramatically he threw his petals forward. Let me tell you, world-renowned Shakespearean actor Michael Crater could learn a thing or two about dramatic scenes from this little plant.

Pepperpot stretched out and sighed annoyingly.

"What's with the fur ball?" Rotsen asked suspiciously as Pepperpot raised her head, sniffed him, then flopped her head back on the bed.

I ignored him as I pulled back the cover and climbed into bed. The comforter was aptly named as I was greatly comforted by it. It doesn't matter how hot it is, I could be in the tropics, instead of rainy old England, but I still need something over my shoulders.

"Oas, we have to figure out what we're going to do. Hello, you do remember our goal is to get back home," Rotsen commanded.

I settled in and opened the paper. Scanning the headlines, there appeared to be nothing earth shattering. A large picture showed the traffic snarls around

Rockhedge Circle, not helped by the construction delays. A smaller picture showed a minor royal looking at an orchid. I guess a flower is more important than welcoming me and my friends to their country. Whatev!

"Right, just let me have a little nap here and we'll talk when I wake up," I said, already asleep by the time Rotsen answered, if he ever did.

Chapter 19

I awoke to a warm wet tongue licking my face. Ahh, what a way to wake up. Scratching behind Pepperpot's ears, she rolled over on her stomach and let out a deep sigh.

"April, dinner will be ready in five minutes," David said as he knocked on the bedroom door.

"Thanks." I stretched my arms over my head, hitting the brass frame by accident. "Geez, I thought he'd let me sleep longer than fifteen minutes," I grumbled. "What a host!"

"Duh," Rotsen never one for flattery stated. "You've been asleep for two hours. That mongrel and I passed the time playing poker. Did you ever see that painting where the dogs are playing cards? It's on black velvet and a real classic. I must remember to try and get one before we head home."

"Yeah, getting you first class artwork to take home is a real priority." I laughed. "Besides, how are you going to carry it?"

"You look really pretty today," Rotsen smoothed me. "Have you lost weight?"

"Are you kidding me? Do you really think I lost weight?" I knew he was trying to suck up to me, but I was going to play it for all it was worth. Besides, I knew the picture he was talking about, I'd seen it at Jezebel's house and I knew if I asked her she'd tell me where she bought it.

"You're just like Twigster."

Yeah right! I looked as much like the famous model from the 1960's as Rotsen did a red rose.

Ignoring him, I used the bathroom attached to the bedroom, freshened up, brushed my teeth, which I have to tell you is a new and exciting earth experience. On Zorca-twenty-three, in my praying mantis form, I don't have teeth like yours and I find it quite a unique experience to have pearly white objects in my mouth. Also, the little brush and tube of gel squirted in one's mouth is like a jet of mint when you least expect it. I'd heard visiting a dentist isn't the best earth time, so I was going to avoid it at all costs. Though I haven't seen a dentist yet in England, so maybe I was safe on that count.

I went back into the bedroom, ran a hairbrush through my locks, and glanced down at the top of the dresser. On it was a pen beside a guestbook.

Being nosy, I couldn't resist. I flipped through the book, drool almost dripping out of my mouth as I spotted familiar names who'd visited the church.

Sir Benton Bronson wrote: Thanks for inspiring me. Your hand-pressed virgin olive oil was the best ever.

Sir Adom John: David, Crocodile Winery had the best red wine I've ever tasted.

Melanie Brownlee: David, Thanks for telling me what you really want, what you really really really want for breakfast.

"Dinner's ready," David bellowed.

"I'm sorry; I had to flip through the book. Do you know how much you influenced history?" I sat down at my seat at the table, Pepperpot settling herself at my feet.

"Aww, you're embarrassing me. They're just friends of mine who stayed in your room. We were just having some fun." He lifted a tray out of the small oven, the smell of fish and chips hitting me like a tidal wave.

"Sir Benton Bronson slept in my bed," I said, nodding as he asked if I wanted chips as well.

He dished out fish and chips onto my plate. "Quite a while ago and I have changed the sheets since then."

I burst out laughing—one thing I seem to do a lot of with David and also with Michael, once I got over the nervousness of being in such supreme company. "You're too funny."

"He sure is a wit," Michael agreed sitting at the table, unfolding a linen napkin, and placing it across his lap before drenching his fish and chips in ketchup. "That's what's so great about him. No matter what kind of day I had at work, when I come home, he always gets me laughing."

"That's all part of the job description." David piled chips on his own plate, then sat down and joined us. "There's ketchup there, salt in the shaker and there's malt vinegar in the glass bottle there."

Famished, I dug into the food. Washing it down with the ice-cold water from a carafe in front of me, I had to ask. "So, tell me your favorite story about a Shakespeare play."

"Surprisingly enough, it wasn't the Scottish play that can't be named but another one. I played the lead part and as a Moor, my makeup was black and it was before the days that they used darkened face cream, so in the heat, it kept melting and dripping. It colored everything, a royal mess." He chuckled at the memory. "But the funniest part I played was a King in Sirlot."

"Oh gawd, that was so funny." David laughed. "They were short of players during opening night, so I had to play his assistant, so I had to make the sounds of the horses' hooves with coconuts."

"I love the man dearly, but he has no sense of rhythm. The horse sounded like he had a broken hoof." Michael smiled. "The audience began to keep the rhythm to help us out. All in all, it was a fun time."

"Yeah, it was like seeing a movie where everyone throws toast at the screen. It was real audience participation," David said. "What can I say? I'm a painter, not an actor."

"David, I saw your artwork in the alley and you're awesome." I gestured to the plate. "Not to mention, a fantastic cook. The dinner was delicious." My plate was empty, and I didn't even remember eating anything.

"He's mine, little lady." Michael poked me in the arm. "But I agree totally. He is a great cook and because of that, I'm taking the dogs for a walk after dinner." At the words, five pairs of ears perked up and the dogs all got up and sat in a straight line by the door.

"Why don't you two go for a walk and I'll clean up?" I offered. "Leave it to me."

I didn't mean to push them out the door, but like a bullet shot out of a rifle, they had the dogs leashed and the door opened.

"Why don't you come with us?" David asked, but without conviction. "We can clean up when we get back."

"No, I insist." I threw a tea towel over my shoulder

and shooed them out the door. Even Pepperpot, the traitor, was on a leash. So much for loyalty. "Now go and have a nice time together. I'll look after the clean-up. Take your time."

"Thanks, April."

"Don't mention it." I shut the door and watched until they were safely down the street. "Rotsen, I need help."

Chapter 20

"I feel like a genie, only summoned from the bottle when I'm needed," he fumed. "I'm not happy with this." He folded his petals and said in a grumpy tone, "Look at this. Cold French fries, cold as a frigging New Zealand winter." He threw down the potato piece in disgust. "What does your majesty need now?"

Geez, someone was suffering from major jet lag. Sweetly, like sugar would melt in my mouth, I did what I do best. I groveled. Big Time. "I sent David and Michael out for a walk and I'm facing a whack of dishes I need to wash." I shrugged my shoulders. "You know I'm no domestic goddess, and I need to know what I'm supposed to do now."

"You a domestic goddess?" Rotsen bent over in half in laughter. "Oh goodness, I can't even get a mental picture of that in my noggin. Well, you can fill that hole with water, squirt in dishwashing liquid, wash them all with the scrub brush there. Then you put them on the drying rack and, using that towel you so conveniently are using as a scarf around your neck, you dry them off."

"Or... You made it sound like I have another choice." I was hopeful. It did sound like an awful lot of work. I mean, why not toss out the plates when they got dirty and buy more? Look at the water you'd save, and everyone knows water is a very valuable commodity.

"Nope, can't think of any way of getting out of the work, nope, nada. You're going to have to buckle down and give it some old-fashioned elbow grease." Calmly, he flipped himself in front of the cupboards, leaves crossed.

"*Fine!*" Without once looking at him, I followed what instructions I could remember, in the order I remembered. So, who cares if I added the liquid before I added the water and that the water was so hot, I had to use pink doctor gloves that were hanging on a pipe under the sink? I had enough soapy suds I felt like I was having a bath and in fact, quite enjoyed the experience. Well, no, not really. I mean, what teenage femawl, alien or humanoid, actually enjoys doing chores. Certainly not me. But I felt like I owed David and by an extent, Michael for putting a roof over my head and a warm bed to sleep in. Yum, the thought of the bed was enough to make me hurry through the rest of the task.

I finished putting the last dish away. I have to admit I was totally pleased with myself. I'd taken on an Earthly task and finished it to a successful conclusion. In the immortal words, I'd done good.

I thought about putting the kettle on as they say when I heard the front door open. "Are you guys back already?"

There wasn't an answer, not the familiar scraping of dog's toenails on the slate floor.

I poked my head around the wall and stood stock-still.

"What the heck are you doing here?"

Chapter 21

"I came for your birthday," Ralb said, setting his suitcase down on the floor. "You do realize it's tomorrow, and I wanted to give you this." He held out a clumsy wrapped present.

"Thanks." I took it from him. "What's with the Santa Claus paper?"

"It was on sale," he admitted sheepishly. "Are you here by yourself?"

As if they were being called, the men appeared at the open door. "April, how come we leave you alone for half an hour and you're entertaining strange men in our home?" David smiled as he unhooked all the dogs and hung the leashes on a hook by the door. "I'm David Stanford and this here is Michael…."

"Crater!" Ralb burst out in glee and I have to say I was embarrassed. How uncool and uncouth was that?

"Calm down, Ralb," I ordered as I backtracked into the kitchen. Grabbing Rotsen, I stuffed him into my pocket. I went back and joined the three men again, Pepperpot nipping at my toes, so I picked her up and she licked my face. "Guys, I admit he is strange, but he's my brother, Ralb."

"Well, what do we owe the pleasure?" Michael asked, in a tone which conveyed anything but pleasure.

"I'm sorry to barge in without calling." Wow, Ralb actually sounded humbled. I wonder what show he'd learned that from. Kind of hard to call as well when one doesn't have a phone. "But well, it's my sister's birthday tomorrow and I brought her a present."

"What? You didn't say anything about having a birthday tomorrow." David punched me lightly on the arm. "This calls for a celebration and just before the summer solstice."

"Really! Please! Don't go to any trouble. Really I mean it." I shot Ralb a dagger-spiked look. "We don't celebrate birthdays in my family and I'd just rather forget it."

"Nonsense. Now, where are you staying?" David asked, leading us all into the family room. "We don't really have any room here, but there is a pull-out chesterfield in the library you can use."

"Or I'm sure he'd be more comfortable at Jezebel's." Michael looked at me and winked. "I'll ring her now."

Gawd! I loved that man.

Chapter 22

"There. It's all settled. You can stay at Jezebel's. She's right across the street and you won't feel like heading back to Jocko's after the night we're going to plan for your sister."

"Thanks, I appreciate it." Ralb smiled at me. "You sure have nice friends."

That I do and I hope you enjoy your stay at Jezebel's.

"So how come you got booted out of Jocko's place?" Michael asked, masking the cutting-edge question with a smile. "Not that I don't think you and your sister are close, but everyone falls out with Jocko sooner or later. Really, I'm surprised Freaky Freddie has lasted as long as he has."

"I might have compared his music to that of Kat KKerry. I thought it was a compliment. Who doesn't like her 'California Beaching song?"

David burst out laughing. "You never compare a dude to a chick. No matter how good the bird might be." He wiped his eyes. "I haven't forgiven him for his comments on my paintings."

"How could he not like the alley?" I asked, genuinely surprised. "It's beautiful."

"Well, thank you." David settled back into the flowered cushions. "But it was more the ceiling of their flat I was referring to. I painted it all in a fortnight, so it would be done when he came back from their New Zealand tour and I never got a thank you."

I nudged Ralb who was parked beside me on tall stools, Pepperpot contently in my lap. "You painted it?"

"I did and I never got so much as a thank-you. That shows you friendship."

"Probably because Hildy took the credit for it," I whispered to Ralb, but I had a more important question in my mind. "How or rather where did you get the ideas for the ceiling?"

"From stories my grandfather used to tell me. He'd often come to babysit me when my mother and father went to see musicals and plays in London. Even when I got older and I wanted to go, I held out for my grandfather coming and going with us, just so I could hear his stories in the tube on the way there and back."

"Your grandfather told you stories about those big uniquely shaped trees, filled to the brim with dripping fruits, each branch a different variety?"

"Yes. Remind me later to show you a picture of us together, but first and foremost, we have to plan April's birthday party. I know we hardly know you, but we're British and love a party." He looked over at Michael. "Any suggestions?"

"Circus themes are always popular. We could rent horses, clowns, and shut down the street." He must have seen the anguish pass across my face. "Or maybe not. Is it an important one? You don't look old enough for twenty-one."

"Thanks, but no it's not an important year and Jezebel might get ideas of standing on the horses with her mom's circus background." Michael nodded and I continued in my head. Michael, dear. You have no idea.

I've passed twenty-one so many times I'm dizzy. If I told you the truth as to how old I am, we'd have to perform CPR.

"Every birthday is special, so what's your favorite kind of cake?" David asked, whipping a pad of paper and pen from under the seat cushions. "What? I like to make lists."

Without hesitation I answered, "Chocolate." How can any Earthling mawl or femawl like anything else other than chocolate? It's definitely a gift from the gods and I know for sure it is. "With chocolate icing."

"Any special decorations you like?"

"David has taken an inkling to the American show, Cake Chief, and I have to say he's been quite successful." David's face reddened at Michael's praise. "He made one for a Prince with his polo team. The horses were so lifelike; he even put a couple of horse patties in the field."

"That was fun." David agreed.

"Surprise me." But on second thought, dealing with Ralb for so many years I felt I should clarify my thoughts. "But please be kind."

"Of course, what kind of dolt do you take me for? Only a complete moron would take advantage of you and embarrass you in front of your friends." I liked his words and how he stared at Ralb the entire time he spoke. "I already know what we're getting you." He leaned over and whispered in Michael's ear, who nodded.

"On that note, let's get Ralb over to Jezebel's and we'll get him settled in." David pushed himself up off the sofa and headed toward the door.

Ralb and I followed and as I cradled Pepperpot in

my arms, she didn't even awaken. I could so see myself becoming a Parental Being, if my kids were as cute and well-behaved as this dog.

After checking both ways and waiting patiently for two bicycles both steered by grey-haired men with clips holding their pants tight to pass. The familiar tingle greeted us as we opened the gate and walked through.

"So is Jezebel hot?" Ralb couldn't resist asking.

"You could say that." David smiled at me. "Sizzling hot, wouldn't you say, April?"

"Very." I should have been worried about leaving my brother in her clutches, but to be honest, I figured whatever she dished out, he deserved, and if he spent a sleepless night, oh well.

David knocked on the door and after about a five-minute wait, the door opened. Ralb's hostess had a bright red hairdo, the hair piled so high a beehive could have fit under it and there still would have been room for the queen bee. Bright red lips highlighted her face, accenting two red circles on her cheeks and black painted-on eyebrows.

"Hi, is Jezebel home?" Ralb asked, looking over her shoulder, into the darkened interior.

"I'm Jezebel, you silly goose, come in, you hunk." She grabbed Ralb's arm and hauled him inside. He stumbled after her and glanced nervously back over his shoulder at me. I took one for the team and shrugged.

David and I stepped just inside the door, whereas Ralb was already halfway down the hall. "Look at the picture on the wall, isn't it cute?" I nodded toward the dogs playing cards.

"Thank you for noticing. I got it at a boot sale," Jezebel said, not loosening her grip on Ralb. I think she saw the look of confusion on my face. "We call them boots, but I think the Americans call them trunks. Anyway, it's a one of a kind."

Disappointed, I spoke. "Oh, that's too bad. I have a friend who really likes that style of art." Oh well, Rotsen would have to find another Earth souvenir for his collection.

"Hey, Jezebel, we're having a birthday party tomorrow for April. Michael and I would like you to come."

"Are you going?" she asked Ralb, stroking his arm, much in the same way I did with Pepperpot.

"Yes, of course, I'm going. She's my sister." Sure, now when it's convenient he wants to admit he knows me. Any other time he acts like we're strangers and personally I like it that way too.

"Great! Say around six o'clock," David stated, clapping his hands. "I have to go and get the cake ready."

Pepperpot squirmed out of my arms and ran over to Jezebel, nudging the pocket of the woman's housedress.

"You are a scamp." Jezebel released Ralb's arm to give the dog a treat out of her pocket. Quicker than you can say quicker, she was back attached to Ralb.

Pepperpot led the way out the front door, stopped for a quick squirt in the flower garden. I prepped myself for Jezebel's disapproval, but my brother must have still been in her sights because she slammed the door shut with her foot and I could hear a little scream from inside. Hopefully, it was Ralb's.

"Don't worry, her bark is worse than her bite," David reassured me.

"Thanks, but I'm not worried about Pepperpot." I

glanced back towards the door.
  "Neither was I."

Chapter 23

"Okay," David said when we were back across the street. "I need you to stay out of my way, so I can get things done for tomorrow."

"Really, please don't go to any trouble," I begged, tugging my sweatshirt further down over my jeans. "I don't want you to do any work."

"You're going to head into the library, the third door on the left, and amuse yourself with the books in there," he ordered. "There's a telly in there if you get bored, but I don't want to see you for at least an hour."

"It's only going to take an hour for you to make my cake." I laughed. "I'm very impressed."

"Heck no, I have to run to the store and get the ingredients. Do you want anything?" He pulled on a jacket, made sure there was his wallet in the pocket, and then wrapped a scarf around his neck.

"Maybe some Cluby bars." For some reason, I had a real craving for the chocolate wafer bars.

"Done, now go in there and relax."

"Done." I reached over and kissed his cheek. "Thanks for being my best Earth friend ever."

He pinched my cheek. "You're welcome and you're very cute. Too bad my heart belongs to another."

"And mine too," I admitted.

"That sounds like a story for another day," he replied, opening the door into the library. "Oops, sorry,

Pepperpot." He sidestepped the dog who was right under his feet. "Now find something to do and I'll be back in a jiffy."

"Will do." I laughed as he closed the door behind me. I turned and took in my temporary prison if one could call it that. I felt like I'd died and had my own version of tree pots. Books to me were like bundles of adventures. When you picked up a book, whether it be a *mist book*, e-book, paperback, or hard cover, it's like you're on a ship, not knowing where the author is going to take you, where he's captaining you to! I ran my fingers over the spines and inhaled the scent of the leather. I really don't know why stars who always put their names on perfume haven't thought to bottle the smell of books. I should mention it to Suzzy, she'd have a sure winner on her hands.

The library had so many books. There was even a ladder with wheels and, of course, I had to try it out. Pepperpot quickly jumped up on the plush chair covered in red peony fabric, turned around three times, and laid down

"How old are you?" Rotsen asked, shimmering out of my pocket just before I climbed aboard the ladder, sailing around the room, almost running into the bow and arrow attached to the wall.

"Whee," I called out, swinging on the ladder, only holding on with one hand. "I can fly."

Pepperpot lifted her head up and flopped it back down.

"Would you find a book and get down from there? I don't want you to hurt yourself," Rotsen ordered. "Pick one out for me, too, since you're already there."

I grabbed two from the top shelf and climbed

delicately down. I hadn't realized how high up I was and was glad to get my feet back on terra firma.

"So, what did you get me?" Rotsen asked, with kid-like eagerness. He climbed up the side of the chair and snuggled into Pepperpot's collar.

"*How to Weed Free Your Garden.*" I laughed as I handed it to him. "And for myself, I got *UFO's: Fact or Fiction.* This should be good for a laugh." I flipped through the book and was surprised to find a picture being used as a bookmark halfway through. Wondering where the picture was from, I read the writing on the back.

David and Grampa 1980

I flipped the card over excited to see what David looked like as a little boy. I could just imagine him with a little cricket bat (I know, I thought it was something to do with insects as well.) and those cute white pants they wear.

The picture flew out of my hand, and I dropped the book on the floor.

"What the heck happened to you?" Rotsen asked, busily flipping through his own book. "Are you okay? You look like you've seen a ghost."

"Rotsen, look at the picture."

I watched as my dandelion wilted and even Pepperpot realized something was wrong.

"Oas, what is David doing with your mawl Parental Being?"

Chapter 24

"I don't know." I searched my brain trying to think of anything David mentioned about his grandfather. I was drawing a blank.

I heard the front door close and David called out. "Okay, I'm back now but don't come out."

"Like heck I won't." I reached for the door handle and pulled it open. "David, I have to ask you a question."

"Sure, ask away, but stay where you are. I'm sure anything you want to ask me can be asked from across the room." He put the groceries out onto the counter and when the carry bags were empty, he folded them and tucked them under the sink.

"Tell me about your grandfather." I know my request was random, but I was impatient and had to find out the info.

"Well, he was an archeologist who loved to travel. I remember running to the Royal Mail when he was away because he'd always send me a special treat. I got stacking dolls from Russia, and not only did I get miniature pyramids from Egypt, I also received a golden dog which he swore came from a famous tomb. It was given to him; it wasn't like he stole it or anything." He turned defensive. "Why do you ask?"

I debated whether to tell him the truth or not, but decided I needed to come clean as they say. "I found a picture of you and your grandfather in one of the books."

"Great! I probably used it for a bookmark and forgot where I put it."

"So, it's special to you?"

"Yeah, it is. One day, he disappeared. I never saw him again. I miss him like crazy." He stopped and wiped a tear from his eye. "You know, I feel a connection to you. I feel like I knew you the minute I saw you at Jezebel's. Almost like we were related." He stopped. "I know, I'm an odd duck."

"No, you're not odd. If you are, then I am too. I felt the same connection, the same vibrations as you." Purposely I strolled across the room and hugged him. I don't know if it was the time or the place to tell him his grandfather was actually the father of six hundred praying mantis' on Zorca-twenty-three. It wasn't really the type of thing you tell a person unless you're three sheets to the wind, and I was too young to drink.

There are some secrets you keep because you love someone enough to want to protect them and this was one of those times. It would be Rotsen's and my little secret and I think Pepperpot would keep her jaws tightly shut as well.

Chapter 25

"Wake up, birthday girl."

I stretched, Pepperpot groaned, and instantly I was wide awake, the mixed aroma of coffee and bacon mingling attractively through the room. The sun shone brightly through the stained-glass window casting a rainbow of colors across the room and onto the opposite wall.

I struggled to sit up, as David placed a tray across my lap. He reached behind me and fluffed up my pillows. With a flourish he flung a white linen napkin across my lap.

"I could get used to this treatment." I bit into a piece of toast, cut in rectangles.

"And so you should. It's your birthday, all day long, so make sure that brother of yours treats you right. I don't think he appreciates you. If I had you for a sister, I'd treat you like a queen," he chuckled to himself. "Or at least a princess."

I dipped another piece of toast into an egg where the yellow part was trying to escape off the plate.

"Ring the bell if you need anything," David said, indicating the brass-handled bell beside a steaming cup of coffee. "I'm putting the finishing touches on your cake."

Without another word, he left the room pulling the door shut on his way out.

Rotsen scurried down from his perch on the top of my headboard and settled onto the tray. He sucked up some of the egg with his stem and grinned. "You sure landed on your feet this time."

"That we did," I gently corrected him as to the fact it wasn't an "I" situation but rather a "we" one. "Yum, you should try this raisin toast," I said as I picked up another slice. "It's to die for."

Rotsen looked serious. "What do you make of the picture of your Parental Being and David's grandfather?" As if to clarify what picture he was talking about. Geez, I hadn't been able to think of anything since.

"I don't know. I was trying to remember everything my dad, er, Parental Being said when he told us about Earth, but both he and my mom were very quiet about it. It only came up the one time in conversation I can remember and that was when I was heading to Earth. Zen, my handler sent me over to Xron to get my traveling paraphernalia. I mentioned to Xron that Zen said I needed some T-gene pills and he said, and I quote, 'Personally I don't think you're going to need it.' He floated across the room, muttering under his breath. 'One thing she doesn't need is more attitude. Must be all those Earth genes hitting an overdrive button.'"

"Well, I could see how you wouldn't pick up on that. Geez, you'd have to be a frigging detective to figure out his thoughts."

"No kidding. He also tends to mumble quite a bit, so usually I just nod and smile where he's concerned."

I don't know if he was being ironic or not but Rotsen nodded and smiled.

"Then when we met up in France with Josh and my Parental Beings, they admitted they had met on Earth but that they wanted to live on Zorca-twenty-three. Can you imagine anyone turning down this place to live on our planet?"

"So says the femawl who can't wait to get back to said planet." Rotsen grabbed a piece of bacon, ripped off a piece for himself, and handed the remaining strip to Pepperpot.

"But that's the only times it's been mentioned. I can't believe it. He had a whole life before he became my dad, er, Parental Being and never said a word." I sipped at the coffee. "What kind of person keeps it secret that he went inside Pyramids and…"

"How we doing in here?" David opened the door a crack and popped his head inside. "Do you need your coffee warmed up or anything else?"

"No, I'm good, but why don't you come in here and sit for a bit. I'd like to learn more about your grandfather." By way of explanation I continued, "I think it's fascinating all the places he's been. He must have been an amazing storyteller. What was your favorite one?" I patted the side of the bed for him to sit and Pepperpot shifted over.

"Umm, that's a tough one." David stole a piece of bacon and tore it up in little pieces for Pepperpot. "Let me think. He was a huge believer in life on other planets and we'd have very strong debates about it." David giggled. "I liked to play the devil's advocate just to get his goat."

I had no idea what he was talking about with devils and goats, but I wanted to learn more about my dad's life on Earth. "For example….."

"Okay, one of the ones we had a lot of fun with was the chalk drawings in England. Have you heard about them?" He continued when I shook my head. "Well, the famous one is called the Dorset Giant. And what they are, are huge chalk drawings on the hillsides. There's lots of them around England and even Scotland. Some of them you can only see from airplanes, hence the reasoning behind that they were made by aliens."

"That and crop circles," I said as I sipped at my now cold coffee. But I wasn't going to complain or ask for a warm-up, I wanted him to finish his story.

"Crop circles, no, those are definitely made by jokesters, but anyway getting back to the Giant." He got up off the bed, reached over to the dresser, and took the pen that sat beside the guest book, which I'd returned after dinner last night. "Have you signed this yet?" I shook my head. "Well, make sure you do before you go." He flipped to the back of the book and drew a picture of a man with two very big clubs.

Quickly I took the book and wrote in my best handwriting before handing it back to him: Thanks for taking me in, you're like family. Love April.

"So, this drawing is on a hillside in England and has been since the 1600's. Reference to it was even found in the town's book where John Zorcan was paid three pounds to add chalk to the ditch." David said, smiling as he flipped to where I'd written in the book. "I feel the same way about you."

"Wait, you lost me, I thought you said it was a drawing, how come there's ditches involved?"

"These are humongous drawings. The Giant for example is over one hundred and ninety feet high on the hillside by one hundred and sixty-seven feet wide. The tool he holds in his hand is one hundred and twenty feet long. Needless to say, it can't just be a line drawn by chalk. To make these outlines, there are gutters, each of them a foot wide and a foot deep." It seemed like a light bulb went off in his head. "Wait here. I'll be right back."

I filled the time stroking Pepperpot's ears. John Zorcan, was it too much of a coincidence that my Parental Being came from Zorca-twenty-three. But he wasn't here in the 1600's or was he? Did he travel back and forth staying for six months at a time? And why was he drawing pictures of giants and horses? Didn't he have better things to do with his time and energy? He was always telling me to get out and do something, and here he was doing stick drawings with chalk. My mind couldn't get itself wrapped around the implications of it. Math for sure wasn't my strong suit and I didn't want to try and figure out just how old my Parental Being was. I mean, everyone thinks their parents are old, but come on, that was just ridiculous. Though I have to admit, he didn't really have a lot of stamina when it came to playing with his offspring. Maybe if my Parental Beings would have stopped at oh I don't know, three hundred instead of going for a record-setting six hundred plus, but I wasn't going to go down that familiar road again.

"Here, take a gander at this." David shoved a book on top of the tray. "Rather than me trying to explain it, they say a picture is worth a thousand words."

"Wow, your drawing didn't do it justice," I said, the words out of my mouth before I remembered I was talking to a real artist. Embarrassed, I could feel my face turning red, starting at my neck upwards. "I mean…"

"It's okay, I know what you mean. Besides, I'm a details man myself." Excited he turned the book sideways so we both could see it. "Look at the countryside and how small it is in comparison to the Giant." Indeed, a real live man stood in the trench by the Giant's club and he was dwarfed. "My grandfather believed it was created by aliens."

"What was his argument?"

"He claimed he had proof, said he found a tool beside one of the trenches that man wouldn't have used in the 1600's." David reached into the pocket of his sweatshirt and pulled out an object, a slightly rectangle book made of brown cardboard.

"It doesn't look like a tool," I said, flabbergasted he held such a unique object in his hands.

"Oh, there you two are." Ralb poked his head inside the open door to my room. "Let me tell you, that was quite the experience staying the night with Jezebel. The stories she told were out of this world. Did you know she was a fan of Tom Jomeys the singer, and went to every one of his concerts? She claimed he has more of her underwear than she does." Ralb glanced at me, then down at the object in David's hands. "What are you doing with a *mist book*?"

Chapter 26

"What are you doing with a *mist book*?" Ralb repeated as each of his eyebrows rose in question. Then, in typical brotherly fashion, he continued, "Hey are you done with that food? I really can't believe I'm hungry after all she fed me."

I had to get the topic off the *mist book*. To David, it was a book his grandfather found, to us, a traveling bible. As I was about to knock the entire tray on the floor, David developed a fit of giggles.

Ignoring the *mist book*, his eyes sparkled. "I know, Jezebel really packs a spread. And speaking of spreads, I should get back to work on our dinner for tonight."

With a flourish, he picked up the tray and headed out the door, leaving the *mist book* on the corner of the bed. "Pepperpot, come on and I'll give you some bacon."

The dog jumped off the bed like it was on fire and after she left the room, Ralb shut the door.

"Explain to me what happened here? Why did you give him our *mist book*? How do you plan on us getting home? What if we have problems or questions we have to solve before we reach Zorca-twenty-three? What if…"

"Shh, he'll hear you," I warned. "I didn't give it to him, he got it himself." I reached under the covers and pulled out the picture of our Parental Being and David.

"Look at this!"

"Great, it's a picture of a young David and our Parental Being." He stared at me, then back to the picture. "Okay….why……is there a picture of a young David and our Parental Being?"

"I found this photo in a book I was reading. I asked David about it and he was telling me and Rotsen, but he didn't know Rotsen was in the room of course, because that would really freak him out if he thought I was planet traveling with a dandelion."

"Anyway…….."

"So anyway, I asked David and he said it was a picture of him and his GRANDFATHER." I waited a heartbeat for dramatic effect. "Ralb, do you know what this means? David's grandfather is our father, our Parental Being."

"How?"

I explained to him my theory and he nodded. "Sounds feasible, except for the part about the Giant. Why did he bother doing all those chalk drawings? What was the point?" He smirked. "Though that would be just like him to do a model of a fertility god based on himself."

"Exactly, and David said his grandfather traveled all over the world, went into Egypt, into pyramids."

"Maybe it's just a coincidence, maybe they just look alike. You know DNA and all that."

"True, maybe you're right. The guy who had the job of filling up the trenches with chalk, his name was John Zorcan."

"Major league crap."

Chapter 27

"My thoughts exactly." I climbed out of the bed and began pacing the room. "What should we do? Should we let him know or keep the secret ourselves?" Again, I paced, caught a glance of myself in the mirror over the dresser and cringed. "Stars! I look rough." It was one thing for Ralb to see me in this state, I mean, he was a long-time relative and all but for David a new relative to see me like this was unacceptable.

"Why don't you go and get changed and we'll talk properly. It's hard to think straight when I keep seeing you flouncing by in your pajamas."

"Fine." I grabbed a T-shirt, shorts, underwear, and a bra from my *hanaglug* and headed into the washroom. I turned on the taps and jumped in. I was still reluctant to enter under the indoor waterfall after my first experience at my friend Nicola's house. Let's just say in the battle of the jets, the jets won. But I persevered and soon got the hang of the taps, knobs, and water sprays. I was victorious, and even though I was now standing in front of British plumbing, I took command and adjusted the knobs a little hotter. I really shouldn't say jumped in, it was more like climbed in over and into the deep bathtub. I've never seen such a deep tub. It wasn't like it was larger than Nic's but it was so deep, I bet you could almost dive off the side and hit bottom. Not that I'd recommend it at all, you could really cause yourself some major brain damage and I needed all the cells I had.

I dried myself off with a fluffy white towel and waited until I was out of the tub before I turned the contraptions off. I'd learned that the hard way when I was at Nic's and got a shot of freezing cold water.

I applied deodorant and got dressed, still impressed by whoever on your planet invented the brassiere. One of these days, when I had nothing to do, I was going to question it on a computer. What an amazing invention to prevent your breasts from bobbing around. Not that mine were big enough to put an eye out or anything if I did move suddenly, but it's always nice to know my deadly weapons were harnessed.

"I thought you were going to try and make an improvement on how you looked," Ralb said, sitting on the side of my bed.

Ignoring him, I headed to the dresser and ran a comb through my wet hair. I put on a bit of make-up, more to accentuate what I have than to make myself look good for any mawl. My heart belonged to only one and I knew I'd never see him again.

But I wasn't going to go there, be sad, wish for what might have been. It was my birthday, and we were going to celebrate it with my new Earth friends.

"So, do you think we should tell David the truth?" Ralb asked, bringing me once again down to Earth.

"Tell me the truth about what?"

Chapter 28

Warily I looked over at Ralb, but I should have known better. When has he ever been able to think quickly under pressure? When has he been able to get our butkis out of a sling when we needed him most? It's been Rotsen who's saved us. Yes, sad but true our race has had to rely on the brains of a dandelion to help us and once again he came through.

"We were planning on doing some sightseeing today if that was okay with you?" Rotsen telepathed me as I spoke the words aloud. "Tomorrow is the summer solstice, and we'd like to go to Rockhedge Circle, but I'd like to see some of the local sights today."

"That sounds great. I can give you a list of places to see. What perks your interest?" David, being British, was proud of his country's history, at least from the tone in his voice.

"What was your grandfather's favorite place?" I asked without thinking. I knew the answer before he even spoke the words.

"English Museum," we said as one.

"How did you know?" David asked, leaning against the door. "Come on and I'll get you the directions."

"Great, a museum," Ralb whined. "Can't we go somewhere fun? I don't care if it is your birthday, I don't want to go to a museum."

"It's not a normal museum," David tried to convince Ralb. "There's the Rosey Stone there, the frieze taken from the Parthenon, and the Window Man. He was found in a peat bog and is over two thousand years old."

"Okay, not to be rude, but the Stone is a hunk of rock, the frieze is more rock, and seeing some old guy's bones isn't really a fun time for me," Ralb admitted. "What girl doesn't want to go shopping." Ralb acted like he was a brainiac and he just came up with the idea of gravity. However, I knew Rotsen had his petal in there somewhere. He was the shopper in the family, more so than me.

"There is an amazing store downtown London called Wrimarket," David said, as he added the directions to the sheet of paper where already he'd written the ones for the English Museum. "It's really easy to get to, just get off the tube at Marble Arch and follow the crowds."

"I don't know if I really want to handle a lot of people on my birthday." I cringed at the thought. "I wanted more of a nice, relaxing, day, say wondering around a museum." I think it would be fun to see the Rosey Stone, it's not like we have anything like that on Zorca-twenty-three. We only speak one language; everyone knows it and it really does make life simpler for everyone involved.

"Why don't we do both?" Ralb pulled at my arm as if he was a little boy. "Come on, let's go. Let's go."

He grinned at David. "I'll keep her out of your hair for the day. You're going to owe me big time."

Picking up the piece of paper, he high fived David and opened the front door. "Sorry, Pepperpot, you have to stay."

"Let me just get my sweater." I ran back into my room, grabbed Rotsen, and slid him under my arm. "Shopping," I hissed at him. "I thought you were my friend."

"Oh, come on," he whispered back. "You need to get yourself a frock for tonight."

"Frock? Frock? Where did you pick up these words from?"

"It's all about the reading, sweetheart, all about the reading," Rotsen chimed as Ralb closed the door.

"Geez, I thought we'd never get out of there. You looked like you were going to spill the beans to him about his grandfather."

"I so would not have. I know how to keep a secret."

We headed side by side down the sidewalk towards the tube station. Funny, how London is. You might have only lived here a week, but in no time at all you felt like a native. No one stares at you or thinks you're odd. You fit right in. The tube stations are very user friendly, and you don't feel embarrassed if you have to stop and ask for directions. But I was an old hand (and foot) at using the system, so I got us our tickets, and we headed towards the moving stairs.

"I got us tickets first for Wrimarket, then we'll hit the museum." Even though it was my birthday, I was an accommodator. I know that for a fact as I took one of those personality quizzes on my *wad* on a day I had nothing to do. Who would have thought someone with a personality like mine—my Parental Being called it strong—would want to make people happy? But I guess it's better than the alternative.

"Great." Ralb looked like he was going to kiss me but obviously thought better of it at the last minute. "I have money, so anything you see is my treat."

We stepped into the arriving train, took seats side by side, and settled in for the journey.

We had the car almost to ourselves, save for a mother with a stroller at the other end of the car.

Figuring I could talk freely, I said, "So tomorrow, we have to get up early, take the tube to Paddingstone Station, then we get on the train to Bath."

"We'll have to get there early to avoid all the crowds," Ralb said, picking up a free newspaper that was on the seat beside him. "Looks like it's going to be packed with people."

"Let me see," I grabbed the paper from him and read the headline.

Twenty-thousand Expected for the Solstice.

If last year was any indication, neighbors of Rockhedge Circle will have a hard time getting out of their own driveways with the amount of traffic expected on the A303 and the A344. Residents near our National Treasure are advised to hang tight during the next few days. Construction expected to be completed on the new motorway to the east of Rockhedge Circle has been delayed due to the constant rains.

"You folks should have already left by now if you're planning on making the pilgrimage." The mother spoke, a young child playing with a key ring in her lap. "It's going to be crazy there and with the bands playing I expect it'll be even bigger."

"Bands? It doesn't say anything about bands." I held up the paper and pointed. "Just the people."

"Don't you folks listen to the radio? It was

announced this morning that Peach Acid and Suzzy are doing their number one song." She picked up the toy the boy had thrown on the floor, wiped it off on her skirt, and then handed it back. "And they're donating their fees to charity. I just hope that lovely lad is feeling better. Word has it he's a tad under the weather."

I stared at her, having no clue as to what she was talking about. What lad was she going on about? Not to be rude, but some people should maybe just stay home with a cuppa tea and not venture outside.

"What should we do?" I asked Ralb as I watched the woman strap the child into the stroller and stand in preparation for the doors to open. "Should we head to Paddingstone now?"

"You can't. You're the star of David's party," he reminded me. "Why don't we do the Wrimarket trip, then head back home, get packed ready to go, then when the party's over, we'll go."

"You sure dodged a bullet there," I agreed with him. "No museum."

"Well, I will take one for the team on that one." He laughed. "Now, I never thought I'd hear myself say this, but let's go spend some of my money."

Chapter 29

And we did.

Big time.

I could definitely get used to spending Ralb's money.

First, if you've never been to Wrimarket, you so have to go and why there aren't any in the United States (I know, I checked), then hop on a plane and get over to England. (Check with your parents first though, I don't want to be held responsible for any immigration problems.)

Imagine a store with floors and floors filled with clothes where you can't believe the price tags. The prices are so low, at first, I thought there must be a misprint. There were purses (my personal favorite thing to buy), shoes, baby clothes (not that I was looking, but always good to know there's stuff there), men's clothes (even Ralb was interested), and woman's clothes. I lost count as to how many floors there were in the store, but everywhere you looked there were shirts, dresses, skirts, sweaters, umbrellas and best of all—there were people to help you. Nothing worse than finding what you like, then no one to help you.

I felt like this store was my own Tree Pot. I found a cute little tiered skirt, the layers of polka-dotted material flowing over the next, and a red cropped shirt. I found jeans, sweaters, and blouses, and headed in the direction of the changing rooms.

"Martha," I read the girl's name tag. I held up a purple sweater I just had to have. "Would you be able to get this in a size two for me?" She was hovering by the doors and before I knew it, she was back with the right size and another one in a pretty pink.

"We just got these in, and I thought it would look jolly well with your coloring."

I took her advice and tried them on, one after the other. The purple one would look really nice with the jeans and the pink one matched perfectly the dots in the skirt. I had two really nice outfits to wear tonight. Now I'd have to decide which one.

Decisions! Decisions!

"Umm, I don't want to bother you, but the girl in the next dressing room just tried this blouse on and it was too small for her." She raised her eyebrows as if to say, what was she thinking. "Anyway, if you'd like another look with the jeans there's this."

She handed me the top, white linen with strings lacing the two sides of each of the sleeves together, reminding me of a bohemian pirate.

I loved it at first sight. I'm not proud to say, I ripped it out of her hands and tried it on.

It was perfect! In more ways than one. It was the perfect mix between peek-a-boo sexy but not slutty, if you know what I mean.

Martha was a great salesperson, a real pet. I wish I could take her home with me. Just like Pepperpot. I'd have to find a lovely going-away present for the cute little puppy. I was sure going to miss her.

"Well, how did it go?" Ralb asked me but kept an eye on Martha. "She's my sister," he explained unnecessarily, "and it's her birthday."

"Happy birthday," Martha said, tidying up the stock someone else had left beside me.

"Thanks for totally embarrassing me," I administered Ralb. "I'm taking all this stuff, but I want to see if I can find something special for Pepperpot."

Directing the next question to Martha I asked her if they had anything for dogs.

"You might try Harrotts or there's a cute little gift shop down the block."

"Thanks, will do." I joined the line-up at the check-out counter. Actually, that's what it was—a great long counter where there were about ten cash registers and the girls behind it all worked right beside each other.

"That'll be sixty-eight pounds," the girl said to me, but winked at Ralb.

He handed over the money and I swore I witnessed a bat fly out of his wallet. It too was probably shocked it saw the light of day.

Remembering my manners, I thanked Ralb and we headed past the guard back out onto the street, joining the throes of people enjoying the passion of shopping in London.

"That was certainly an experience I, for one, would like to forget," Rotsen said, poking his head out. "I think we've unleashed a tigress. For a femawl who doesn't like shopping, you could have sure fooled me."

"Aww, I know someone who needs some caffeine to cheer up." I was already on a high from spending my brother's money. Could the day get any better?

We stopped at Starpunds—how could you not—and I ordered my favorite sweet coffee, with soy. I can't digest milk for some reason, since my space travels, and almost drank it in one gulp. Yum.

"Do you realize we spent as much on one top as you did in this coffee shop?" Ralb moaned.

What can I say? There are those of us on earth who appreciate a fine cup of coffee and those that do not. It's a losing battle trying to convenience a "cheap skate" to spend good money on a good cup. What surprises me most is the fact for a country known for its tea consumption, that there are so many high-end coffee shops. I even heard there was one in the bottom of the *Louvre* in Paris. Different country I know, but really how great was that. One could gaze at that famous painting and then have a cup of Joe and if they were from Zorca-twenty-three actually know why she was smiling.

We wandered the streets, and I don't know about Ralb but I was enjoying the atmosphere of London. A slight rain fell, not drenching but more of a mist, just enough to cool me off and give me a second or third wind for shopping. Stores designated for tourists, with their Union Jack sweatshirts and Kono Street T-shirts rubbed right alongside fish and chip restaurants. I couldn't resist and popped into one and found the perfect gifts for two dear friends.

"Come on, Ralb." I pulled him along. "Let's keep walking and see where we end up."

"Whatever, it's your birthday. As long as I don't have to go to any stupid museum."

"Amen, to that one," Rotsen agreed. "Who wants to spend the day in a musty old museum."

"What do you think our Parental Being found so interesting in there?" Ralb asked as we walked.

"You know what a history buff he is, heck he was

probably around when the Stones were first moved."

"Fine." We walked, and walked, and I was so caught up in the passing architecture, the history, I didn't realize we'd gotten to Harrotts until I saw the familiar yellow awning.

"Harrotts. Can you believe it?" Excited I ran the last few steps, then stopped and waited for him to catch up. "Come on."

I smiled as the door was held open by a doorman. I'm glad we weren't wearing a backpack because people ahead of us were and they got stopped by the doorman. What an important job hc had!

The food area we walked through looked as if we were in a rich person's kitchen. Stained-glass lights outlined the different areas. There was a pizza area where the chef sang as he cooked. Another room contained boxes upon boxes of chocolates, all lined up like soldiers, all perfectly straight. And the smells. If ever there was a heaven on Earth, it was located in this store.

If I ever met Mr. Harrott, I'd definitely kiss him.

"No way am I buying you anything in here." Ralb showed me one of the price tags on a small box of chocolate. Again, I thought there must have been a misprint but not in a good way. Following the crowd, we headed down the Egyptian moving staircase down to the bottom of the store.

Ralb had bypassed the crowds and headed into the sale room. I went over to him and grinned. This was my type of room. There were lots of purses, some with little dogs on them and after pleading it was my birthday after all. I broke him down and he bought me one. I found some dog treats, I couldn't buy for one and not all.

"Come on, enough of this spending my money. We have to get back to the house."

Knowing when to push my luck, I knew all good things must come to an end. I spun around taking in the sights and smells of Harrotts, truly an English constitution.

But enough feeling sad and sorry for myself, it was time to party. And who doesn't like to party when you're the center of attention.

Chapter 30

"Here's the birthday girl now," David called out, wrapping the cord around the vacuum cleaner. "I was hoovering and just finished. You guys came at the perfect time." He glanced down at the bags. "Looks like someone spent some money."

"Yeah, too much," Ralb grumbled. "I need a drink."

"You've come to the right place," Michael said from across the room. "Come over to my bar and I'll make what you want non-alcoholic." Without waiting for Ralb's request, he provided us with a juggling act with bottles and glasses that would have made any bartender proud.

The dazzling display of his was making me dizzy, so I headed into my room and threw my purchases on the bed.

"Our guests are expected in about half an hour," David told me as I came back into the main area. "You might want to get changed now."

"I don't think it's allowed for me to be bossed about on my birthday." I laughed to show I was joking. "Fine, if you're sure there's nothing for me to help with out here."

"Everything has been taken care of, just go and make yourself prettier."

"Well, I guess that'll be one less person at the

party," Ralb said, gulping down more of the pink liquid in his glass. "By the time she makes herself pretty, the party will be over." In case no one got the just of his conversation, he went on to clarify even further. "I mean…"

"We know what you mean, now be nice and help me cut up lemons," Michael advised as he slid a cutting board, knife, and lemons across the makeshift bar.

I didn't wait for my brother's grumbled response. I sank down on the bed, squished up into a ball because of all the bags. I peered around the room, trying to remember as much as I could. In such a short period of time, this room felt more like home to me than any other place I'd visited on Earth, including Nicola's house, my friend from Bedrocktown.

"Now don't you start," Rotsen said, shoving his head out from the top of the Harrott's bag.

"What do you mean? I was just…"

"I know what you were just doing and in about thirty seconds, your eyes are going to fill up with tears, and we're going to have enough water flowing out to flood the Thames." He skittered over to the table beside the bed and grabbed a tissue from a box I hadn't even noticed was there. "You're going to go down the track of thinking how much you're going to miss your new friends and how much fun you had and how you'll never have as much fun ever, ever again."

"I so was not." I hopped off the bed and headed into the shower. I didn't need a two-bit dandelion with as much emotional understanding as a rock telling me what I was feeling. I turned on the knobs, took off my clothes, and stepped into the tub. I was a teenage femawl, it stands to reason I would be sentimental about a place where I had such fun. Who wouldn't be sad to leave England, a place with so much history and so many jolly, lovely people? Okay, like any place there were some bad things about it. I put shampoo on my hair and lathered it up. Smoking was not great. It seemed to be a natural pastime in pubs and one people should probably give up or they themselves would become history.

Ah, the history of England. Amazing to me how in ancient times people in England were building roads and had indoor plumbing and yet in other countries they were living in teepees and hunting animals. While my future Parental Being was drawing grade school pictures with chalk, the Romans had already built viaducts to take water from the sea to their houses. They had indoor plumbing and heated floors. The Roman Baths were an engineering feat and I wanted to see them on the way to Rockhedge Circle. My only regret here was that I hadn't taken the time to visit the museum. Imagine the history between those doors. And it was all free. I should have mentioned that to Ralb and I bet he probably would have changed his mind about shopping. Not that I regretted shopping. I know I sounded like a fickle person, but I always got like that before I traveled.

I added fruity smelling conditioner.

England is great. I mean, if royalty lives here when they could live anywhere else in the world, it must be a wonderful place. Plus under the palace is that secret vault under the castle that's supposed to contain all kinds of interesting museum pieces. How cool is that?

I soaped the rest of my body, running my hands over the parts I'd become so familiar with during my

Earth reign. I would miss my bits and bobs, my skinny waist, which I received thanks to a Black Hole and not any one of the countless diets I see advertised on my *wad*. My butt which I have to say looked very good in jeans, and I'm not being braggy or anything, Josh told me so himself, and he should know. I caught him looking at it more than once when I turned around.

Josh, my poor Josh. My first Earth mawlfriend, who loved me for who I was, not what he could get off me. We shared our first kiss on a rock overlooking Bedrocktown, and I pointed out Zorca-twenty-three. Of course, I didn't tell him I was from there—that came later.

What? I can see your shocked expression now as you're reading this. If you truly love someone, and more importantly, you believe he loves you, you want to be honest with him and furthermore, be honest with yourself. In order to do that, you have to take the step even though your heart is pumping a kilometer a minute. (Hey I'm in England, I have to use the metric system).

And as I knew in my heart-shaped organ (yes, I know it's not really that shape. Geez you guys are as nit-picky as Ralb) he was cool with it. Okay, I might have taken advantage of the situation, we'd landed in France, and really, how can you get mad with someone in France? It's the country of romantics.

Thanks to Ralb, who had to put his two cents in, long story shorter, he saw me in my true form before he switched into a Zorcan praying mantis.

My Josh was willing to accept me, flaws and all. Then something happened. Something that was blown way out of porpoise. He saw me with Beau (the manager of Suzz) and jumped to the wrong conclusion. We parted company in New Zealand and I never saw him again.

Now the tears fell from my eyes and when I stepped from the shower, turned off the knobs, the towel I held in my hand was soaked.

With shaking hands, I wrapped one towel around my head and the other around my body.

"I knew it," Ralb thoughtfully said when he saw me. "You're such a wimp. You don't see me bawling like a baby because I have to leave."

"I was crying because I miss Josh." I wiped my nose on the towel—sorry to be so classless, but I was far from the tissues. "You'd know what I was going through if you'd ever cared for someone other than yourself."

"You make me sound self-centered. If I was, I wouldn't have bought you all those clothes."

Wow, chalk one up for Ralb, the king of guilt trips. Not to mention the prince of turning things around to his own advantage.

"Yes, thank you. Now, why don't you leave so I can get dressed?" I could hear voices outside the door. "You need to get out there and mingle. Did you bring all your stuff from Jezebel's? We need to get going as soon as we can!"

"Right!" What is it with mawls, especially my brother? He can dish out the orders, and then conveniently forget what he himself needs to do. "Be right back."

I ripped off the tags on the skirt and top and put them on. Checking myself in the mirror, I combed my hair, applied make-up, and was GtoG. Funny how fast I was able to get ready. From what I've heard from Suzz, it takes femawls forever.

Reminding myself I had to do what I'd told Ralb to, I shoved my new purchases into my *hanaglug* and slammed the lid shut.

"I think I have everything," I said to Rotsen as we both checked out the room.

"There's your *mist book* on the table."

"Right! What would I do without you?" I asked him, as I added the book to the top of the case. Then I picked him up and tucked him behind my ear. "Come on, we've got a busy night planned.

"Here's the birthday girl now," David and Michael chorused as one. "Here's a birthday drink." He confessed, "I made it without alcohol as I wasn't sure how old you were."

"Old enough to know better, but young enough to still want to do it," Jezebel laughed, raising her glass, and downing the liquid in one. "Fill me up, cowboy."

Ralb entered the house without knocking and headed over to the bar, pouring himself a soda without so much as asking the hosts. Man, where does that boy get his lack of manners?

I did the math on my fingers and in Earth years, today I was eighteen. Quite a bit better than if I was on Zorca-twenty-three where I'd be at least three hundred years old. Guess you could say I looked extremely well preserved.

"I'm eighteen today." Pepperpot rubbed her wet black nose against my leg. "Aww, aren't you cute with your pink bow?" I lifted her up and she immediately began to lick my face and neck. I checked with David and gave the dogs the treats. You'd think it was their birthday. They were so happy.

"Happy birthday," David sang. "Time to open presents."

"Okay," I agreed. I sounded like Ralb, a willing participant in anything where I was the center of attention.

"I'll have to put you down," I said to Pepperpot as I accepted the card from David. "You don't need to get me a card, you've done so much already."

I opened the pink envelope, an exact match to Pepperpot's bow to see a hand-drawn dog holding a balloon, the words "Happy Birthday" on the balloon.

Aloud I read the handwritten poem.

"You've brought laughter and love to our home.

And because of that we nev'r want you to be alone.

A four-legged pal is our gift to you.

We don't want to share any more clues.

Love David and Michael"

Shocked I peered from one to the other, as Pepperpot sat contently at my feet.

"Are you kidding me?" I squealed and ran over to hug both the men at once. "That's the best gift ever." I scooped up my dog and included her in the hug.

"Well, fine," Jezebel fumed. "How am I supposed to top that? All I got you was the stupid picture you liked from my wall."

Again, I squealed. "Not the one with the dogs playing cards."

She nodded; her face split in half by her grin. "I took it out of the frame, to make it easier for traveling." She handed me a rolled-up scroll. "Not that I'd like to lose the pleasure of your brother's company anytime soon, but both of you seem to be wanderers." Her eyes turned misty. "Aww, to be young again. I remember David's grandfather and I used to be quite the sightseers. We filled completely one passport and were working our way halfway through the second…"

"You knew David's grandfather?" I squealed. "Sorry," I said, as I saw David cover his ears. I'd forgotten David had mentioned it before I knew the details. "That was a little too high a sound."

"That's okay, it's your birthday." David went behind his bar again and began to mix more drinks.

I settled onto the sofa beside Jezebel waiting to find the appropriate time to pick her brain, Pepperpot tucked in beside me and sighed. "Geez, does life get any better than this?"

"Yes, when you've tasted my food. Come everyone to the table and we'll get started." David had made place cards, so we all sat down. Leafy salads with tiny tomatoes, cucumbers, and bean sprouts were artistically arranged. Followed quickly by a main course of roast beef, Yorkshire pudding, and little carrots, then the highlight of the dinner—the cake.

"I don't mean to rush you, but we're treating everyone to a train ride to Rockhedge Circle."

I squealed again and a piece of roast beef shot out through my teeth. "You mean all of us?" I glanced over at Ralb and raised an eyebrow. How were we going to ditch these people so we could end up traveling through the rocks?

"But," David continued, "I don't want anyone to think we're all joined at the hip. We can all ride there together, and then head off on our own."

"That's David's polite way of saying he wants to hit the town of Bath and go shopping. Meaning, we probably won't hit the summer solstice at Rockhedge Circle until sunset." Michael punched him lightly in the arm.

"Sounds good, but really, we can't accept you paying for Ralb and me. You've given me a roof over my head, food in my stomach, and the best present ever." Oops, I saw the look cross Jezebel's face. "One of the best gifts," I stuttered and gave her a quick kiss on her rouged cheek.

"Really, I'll pay for it," Ralb said half-heartedly.

Boy, I could muster up more enthusiasm going to the dentist to have all my teeth taken out.

"We'll worry about that later." David placed the cake in front of me, the pink candles blazing.

Okay, I admit it. I squealed again. I really was going to have to stop making that noise. It was really girlish and from what I could see of the faces on my friends, very annoying. But if you saw the gooey concoction, I had placed in front of me, well, you'd squeal as well.

Obviously taking into account how much I love Pepperpot, David's creation was a life-size Westie dog, complete with collar and dog tag. The dog was standing in a mass of green icing, a park-like setting, with a field full of dandelions. The stems were green licorice and swayed in the slight breeze in the room. The effect was amazing, even the trail through the weeds were little chocolate pebbles.

"The entire cake is edible," David said, taking out his camera and snapping a picture.

"I really don't know what to say. This is the most amazing birthday ever." I tried not to tear up, but I couldn't help myself.

"Blow out the candles before all those waterworks put them out anyway," Ralb ordered.

"And don't forget to make a wish."

So, I did. I wished for something I knew I'd never have again because that's what wishes were for, the unobtainable.

"So, what did you wish for?" Ralb asked, accepting the piece of cake with the most icing. Typical.

"She can't tell you or it won't come true." Michael handed me the cake, then a small piece for Jezebel.

I knew it wouldn't come true anyway. I wished for the impossible. I wished for...well, I don't think I can tell you either. Well, I might as well, I guess it wouldn't come true anyway.

I wished I could kiss Josh one last time.

Chapter 31

"Does everyone have everything?" David asked as we waited for the train at Paddingstone Station. We had half an hour to kill before the next train, so I busied myself visiting the Starpunds, upstairs, and then hit the bookstore downstairs. The numerous little stands in the terminal sold everything from orange juice to newspapers to bears based on the name of the station.

It was a hub of activity with trains coming and going. One family, with Canadian flags on their backpacks, were visibly upset. I watched the train conductor (which by the way was very cute and not at all fat) shake his head, then point toward the ticket counter.

"I can't believe we missed the train by three minutes, eh," the Canadian mom said as she passed David and me.

"No matter what anyone says, the British are known for their train schedules. You have to be on time or ahead of time if you want to make it. The trains wait for no one." He glanced down at the designer bag where Pepperpot was being carried. "How's she doing in there?"

"She's fine," I whispered. "Am I going to get a hard time taking a dog into our compartment?" I was torn. If I had to bypass the rock traveling to keep my dog it would be a tough call, but I think I'd stay on

Earth and take the consequences. Funny how this furry little doggie had worked her way into my heart and other body parts.

"First of all, we aren't in a compartment, just seats, some of them are facing forward and some backward."

"I call the forward-facing one," Ralb said, *earsdropping* on our conversation as per usual.

"What are you, like two years old?" I couldn't believe him. We'd space traveled where we'd gone forward and backward, not to mention upside down and sideways, and he's worried about facing backward on a smooth surface.

"I get car sick," he said by way of explanation.

What a wimp, not to mention a major liar.

"I packed a little barf bag, in case my little Ralby gets sicky," Jezebel said, clinging to his arm like he was the last life preserver on a sinking ship.

Good, she could be the clean-up commando on this trip.

Ralb picked up her carry bag decorated with stickers and held onto it. "You're my seat partner."

I turned my head as they began to whisper together. Like get a room. She was old enough to be his grandmother and yet when she smiled, it was like she was a flirty teen.

"And second of all," David continued completely ignoring Ralb (how could you not like this man), "they allow all kinds of animals on the trains."

"So, we shouldn't have any trouble getting Ralb on board then."

"That's a good one, April. You're so funny I forgot to laugh," Ralb pouted. "Gee, where do you get your one-liners from, a caveman?"

"Do I need to separate you two?" David asked, coming to stand between us. "It's a long train ride and I don't want to spend the whole time playing referee."

I burst out laughing, catching the eye of the Canadian mom who came to stand near us after buying their new tickets. "Your dad sounds just like my husband."

"Oh, he's not my dad." I was flattered in a way to think I looked that much like David, but I could tell he wasn't impressed he looked old enough to be my Parental Being.

The woman shrugged and went back to discussing if they'd have enough time to head to Starpunds before their train arrived. Personally, I think there's always enough time for a cup of coffee, but then again I'd been warned about the British trains.

Her two boys were sitting on their suitcases, heads in their hands reminding me of trips I had to take with my Parental Beings. They were bored, no doubt missing their computer games.

"Could I ask a small favor?" A man dressed in a dark brown suit and red tie, a covered birdcage in his hand asked the Canadians.

I had the act down to a science, listening that is without appearing to do so. I tended to Pepperpot's bag, fiddling, but not making so much noise I couldn't hear their words.

"I see you're on your way to Bath and my son is going to University there."

The mother joined in. "I hear it's got a beautiful campus. A fact I keep telling my oldest son Greg," I smiled when the boy, obviously Greg, gave a little wave at the mention of his name, his iPod cords running to his ears. "If he applied himself he could go there too."

"Grace, dear, we promised we wouldn't nag him on our holidays."

"True, Henry dear, but we don't want him to lose focus and turn out like your brother Al."

"Don't start on my family, your family has some odd ducks as well," the father said in a chilly tone.

"Anyway," the suited man broke in, "my son asked if I would mind getting his bird to him."

"So why can't you?" Greg asked suspiciously, his iPod not as loud as I'd presumed.

"Greg, don't be rude."

"No, the young lad has made a valid point," the man agreed. "My second wife, not my son's mother, is sick and I don't want him to think I love her more than him. You know how kids are." He glanced over to the Canadian mother who nodded. "So, would you mind taking the bird onto the train? There's a seat paid for it and everything, so it's no problem. When you reach Bath, just take it off the train. My son will be there on the platform waiting for it."

"What if he's not?"

"He works part-time at the station so take it into the office and they'll know all about it."

"What if there are drugs in there?" Greg asked, lifting the cover of the cage. "We don't want to be arrested in a foreign country for dope running."

"Good point, but it's not like you're crossing the borders or anything," the man sighed. "Never mind, I'll see if I can find someone else to help us."

The family had a quick huddle together and I heard the words, Canadians/nice/helpful/international visitors brandied about.

"We'll help you," the father approached the man, and they shook hands.

"Geez, I hope there's no bomb in the stupid bird," Greg mumbled before adjusting the earpieces back in his ears.

I heard it before I saw the train, its white light shining like a beacon in the darkness. The train whistled into the station, stopped, and each of the doors electronically opened. Businessmen in suits, women in colorful saris, the light material dancing as they walked, disembarked.

It was like a circus clown car, unbelievable how many folks they could fit into such a small, confined space.

"Can we get on now?"

"Sure, our train is right over there," David nodded to a long train on the farthest platform.

"You mean it's been here the whole time and you didn't tell us."

"I thought it would be better for you two to burn off some energy before you got on. It's going to be a long night, and I want you to get some sleep on the train." David picked up the carry bag and I kept Pepperpot in the crook of my arm. "Do you have our tickets?"

Michael nodded and we walked down the long cement walkway to our train.

When we got to the carriage with the number matching our tickets, he handed them to a freckled red-haired man dressed in the same colors as the train. A sky-blue blazer was over a snow-white shirt, tucked into matching pants and brown shoes completed his uniform. I was about to mention to him, not that I was an expert or anything, but I'd spent enough time with Suzz to learn brown doesn't normally go with blue, but then thought maybe it wasn't any of my concern.

"The dog needs to be in the carry-all." The man announced in a loud no-nonsense voice.

I matched up the number on my ticket to the number above the seat and put Pepperpot on the empty space beside me, obediently she crawled into the carry-all and laid down falling immediately asleep.

Aww! Finally, able to sit down, I stretched my legs out and was relieved to see David and Michael across the aisle, Ralb and Jezebel in the row in front of me.

I closed my eyes and relaxed. I breathed in and out, in and out. I didn't want to think about how fast we'd be pummeling along these tracks and how easily the train could pop off.

I unzipped the bag to let Pepperpot have a bit more room and leaned my head against the glass. Finally, we pulled out of the station and the rhythmic movement of the train lulled me to sleep.

"Happy belated Birthday, Oas," sing-songed a voice I recognized all too well.

Startled, I awoke and wiped the water trying to escape from the side of my mouth, off on my sleeve. I must have been dreaming, no one but Ralb knew my Zorca-twenty-three name. I rubbed my eyes and stared out the window at the passing scenery, well what I assumed was scenery, in the darkness it was really just flashing lights.

"Happy belated Birthday, Oas."

It wasn't a dream, more a nightmare and when I turned around and peeked through the crack between the two seats, I covered my hand over my mouth to suppress the scream.

Chapter 32

"What was that?" I heard Jezebel ask.

"Oh, my sister being a drama queen again. Same old, same old, even on her birthday, she can't give it a rest."

"Just zone her out my little Ralby. Would you like something from the food car?" Ralb must have nodded because Jezebel shot me a dirty look as she passed me.

"So, what was that all about?" Ralb asked as he lifted Pepperpot and her carrier onto his lap and slid into the adjoining seat.

"Happy Birthday, Oas." the words repeated.

"Did you hear it? Something or someone just wished me a happy birthday," I whispered to him, not wanting to alert David and Michael to anything being wrong.

"Duh, it is your birthday, so what's so unusual?" Ralb shrugged his shoulders. "You really need to find yourself a mawl."

"Ralb, there's a bird in a white cage behind me and I swear on your life the words came from it. Not only that, Ralb, it called me Oas."

Yawning, he continued. "Duh, it is your name."

"What's with these duh's all of a sudden? Get with the program. I was called by my Zorca-twenty-three name, not my Earth one."

"Oh, right." Jezebel came back along the aisle,

holding enough food to feed ten teenage boys. Bags of crisps were snuggled up against her breasts alongside packages of Cluby bars, and my favorite ChocoCircles. That was really sweet of her to remember the rest of us and our hunger.

"I wasn't sure what you were partial to, so I got everything I could carry." She settled back into her seat and like a lightning bolt Ralb was up and out of the seat.

Guess the only part of those ChocoCircles I'd be seeing is the wrappers when Ralb discarded them on the floor.

"Wish I could help you sis, but the food is calling my name. You'll just have to figure that one out on your own."

At that moment, Rotsen shifted from behind my ear. "Boy, he's really a great guy to count on in time of need."

"You've got it in one. Did you hear what happened?" I asked, glancing out the window, checking the reflection to see if I could see any action happening on the seat behind me.

"Yes, unwind me and I'll head back and see what's going on." I did as Rotsen asked and held my breath as he snuck between the opening separating the seats.

"Want a bag of ChocoCircles?" Ralb asked standing over my seat, the candies an obvious peace offering. Well, he's got another thing coming if he thought a little bag of sweets would "sweeten" my disposition as I yanked the bag out of his hand. "I can't be bought." Now, go away. You're never there when I need you. Go back to Jezebel and her stories."

Rotsen popped his petals over the headrest, a look

I'd come to realize only represented bad news.

"Well?" I asked, as I put three ChocoCircles into my mouth. Nothing bad could happen when you have chocolate in your mouth. "What did you discover? See, that's the difference between you and Rotsen—he's willing to help me out, take one for the team. Put his life on the line to save mine."

"Oh, get over yourself. All he did was put his head under the birdcage covering and see what was going on. That's hardly jumping in front of a bullet or lying down on the train tracks to stop a train from running over you."

"Maybe not, but when have you done any of those things? When I ask you, when?" I popped another couple of ChocoCircles into my mouth, the sweet chocolate melting on my tongue.

"Are you two at it again?" Michael asked. "You're worse than cats fighting."

He was right. It did seem like we were always fighting and even if I did feel I was justified feeling the way I do and saying the things which needed to be said, it really couldn't be pleasant for folks having to listen to us go on.

I ignored him and looked out the window, seeing first of all my own reflection. Then I focused more on the distance toward the lights of the towns we were passing. We stopped quickly at a station, and then picked up speed again. The country stretched beside me, and where once there were towns, now there was darkness.

I looked, and then looked again. A horse on a hill was illuminated, the chalk outline glowing on the hill, the horse's tail high to the left.

I realized Ralb was still standing there, waiting for something, waiting for me to speak.

"Truce?" I asked, once again acting as peacemaker.

"Fine!" He thrust another bag of ChocoCircles on my lap.

"Now you two are all back being friends, would you like to know what I found out?" Rotsen asked, stealing one of the ChocoCircles. He sucked on the candy before continuing. "We've got bigger problems than you two arguing. You'll never guess who was behind curtain number 1?"

"Spill the beans, Rotsen. You've been watching way too many game shows."

A voice announced over the loudspeaker we were pulling into Bath and to please return to your seats.

"Sorry, gotta go." Ralb glanced at me. "What? I'm not dodging the problem, but one must always consider one's safety in these times."

"Of course." Of course, I didn't believe him. Things would never change with my bro. No matter what planet we were on I'd just have to accept the fact he was always looking out for number one—Ralb.

Rotsen glanced left and to the right, before covering his mouth with his leaf and whispering in my ear. "We have to ditch that bird. When the train stops, we have to leave asap."

"The bird isn't our responsibility," I reminded him. "It's the Canadian's job to get it to its destination, to the man's son, not ours."

"Nothing against Canadians, but they might not have realized what a task they are going to have."

"Please, Canadians are tougher than anyone gives them credit for. Besides, it's just a simple white bird."

"It's your old boyfriend, Gorget."

Chapter 33

"Make sure you have everything," Michael reminded us. "Before we left, I reserved us a car. I figured with all the folks coming to this event, we'd never get a taxi."

"Hard to believe you could get a rental, but not a taxi," Jezebel mentioned. "Not that I'm going to mind being squeezed up against this young man's flesh."

"No doubt Michael has a friend who has a friend…" David smiled. "Or maybe a fan."

"True. Actually, he's a big American star who owns property in Bath. I can't tell you who, but let's just say he was in a blockbuster alien movie and we'll leave it at that." Ignoring the names being bantered about, he whipped out his cell phone and punched in the numbers.

"Hi, yep……., yep,.. that's really kind of you…… I owe you." He flipped the phone shut and put it back into his breast pocket of his lightweight jacket. "My American friend is having car trouble, but he's arranged another one for us to use." Without further explanation he continued. "I don't know about you guys but I'm starving. What do you prefer? Tea and scones or noodles?"

We walked along the crowded cobblestone streets, lit by black streetlights. On every corner a different busker entertained. Ralb was mesmerized by the fire-eaters, but I continued on, drawn to the lowly guitar player, strumming his instrument in a forlorn manner, a young boy sitting by a tin can, listlessly dropping each of the three coins back in. The sounds emanating from the strings made it sound like the player had lost his last friend, like a mermaid on the rocks alluring to the sailors.

I pushed my way through to the front (but in a nice non-Ralb way) only to see Jocko and my mouth gaped open in shock.

"Jocko, what's the matter?" This man who last week was living the life of Riley (I for one would like to know who this Riley bloke is), was now dressed only slightly better than a homeless person. His sweater was ripped and appeared to have been in a fight with a family of moths. His jeans were torn and not in the fashionable way the kids were all wearing them. His hair was mussy, greasy and I could have sworn in the lamplight, I saw a bug crawl out.

With half-closed eyes he peered up and smiled with yellowed teeth. I staggered backward, not in shock from his words, but from the rancid odor escaping from his mouth.

Once he'd stopped playing, the crowd moved on to the next freak show and we were left alone.

I knelt beside him, my knees cracking in the unnatural (at least for me) position.

"Talk to me. Tell me what happened. I mean, it was only a few days ago you and Freaky Freddie told me to leave. Not that much could have happened."

"Hildy was not the person we thought she was."

No kidding on that one. If you recall, she was also Gorget, who Rotsen said was the bird in the cage on our train. My ex-mawlfriend certainly got around.

"Are you listening?" Jocko asked snarkily. "Looking back, I think she made up those lies about you to get rid of any competition you might have given her."

I could see that.

"She went to bars every night, came home drunk, brought home 'guests.' Freaky Freddie and I didn't like the looks of some of them and wouldn't allow them in our flat."

"Wow, they must have been rough-looking." Involuntarily I peeked down at his tattoos, a one-of-a-kind artwork on his neck. "One of the girls even had Porcupine-spiked hair. Let me tell you, she was a fright."

"You know how your radar can tell when folks are just bad news, bad to the bone, bad to their very souls, bad, bad, bad." He patted each of his pockets. "You wouldn't happen to have a pen and piece of paper, would you? That sounds like the making of another song."

Ignoring him, I asked him to go on. "On two separate nights, I had to head down to the jail and bail her out." Sure, where the heck was he when I was in the slammer? I could either hold a grudge match, or let my anger go. It was no frigging good to keep it penned it, but I wasn't going to let him off that easy either. "What about the death that was supposed to happen?"

"Geez, don't you listen to the radio?"

"Hildy is gone, Freaky Freddie contacted a major virus and is hospitalized, on death's doorstep." His voice betrayed his mood and once again it was filled with sobs.

"What about Suzz? Did she abandon ship as well?" Wouldn't that be just like her! Slowly I'd developed a liking for her, but in all cases, I should have gone with my first gut instinct. Not to delve back into that but let's just say she and Ralb got along quite well and leave it at that.

"I'm right here," the boy to the left of Jocko spoke. "I'm Suzz."

Chapter 34

Okay, I admit I didn't see that one coming. She always was small, tiny, but if she was going for the twelve-year-old boy without a wash in a week, she'd succeeded.

"What's so interesting over here?" Michael and David joined our group. "I admit this guy can play the guitar." Each of them dropped a handful of coins into the can. "But come on, there's lots more to see and we have to pick up the car."

"Michael, David, this is Jocko and Suzz from the band Peach Acid." I continued. "They are in a bit of trouble. Hildy has left the band." I didn't want to get into details about how now we suspected on good authority (Rotsen) that she was now the bird in the cage. "And Freaky Freddie has fallen victim to a virus and won't be able to play tonight."

"Right, we're set to do a performance at Rockhedge Circle. We got an advance, which we already spent." Jocko moaned. "I won't be able to pay it back."

"What, mate? Did you think you could make enough playing your guitar on the street corner?" Michael asked. "Never mind, we'll take care of things."

"It's a royal mess. I don't know what you or anyone else could do."

Michael was a take charge kind of guy. Maybe

Ralb could learn a few things. "Okay, here's the plan. David is going to fill in singing where you need him, and I've got some friends in Bath who know how to play your kind of instruments."

"Thanks, but it's hopeless. No one will be able to learn the songs in time." Dejected, he picked at the strings of his guitar.

"Quit feeling sorry for yourself." His attitude, of the stiff upper lip bravo, reminded me of two of the British judges on two different reality shows. Those Brits really called them as they saw them, and to heck with your feelings. Must be something to do with all the tea they drink. It's not a scientific fact, I'm just saying.

"Your songs are on the radio a million times a day; anyone could play them." He held out his hand to Jocko. "Come on, we've got a lot to get accomplished."

"How can we help?" I asked, not really knowing what we could do but glad Michael was taking things in hand.

"You, Ralb, and Jezebel head to Rockhedge Circle. The car belongs to a cousin of the royal family. What? My American friend came through for us and I don't mean to brag but when her cousin found out it was for me, er, us, she jumped at the chance. She's a patron of the arts and loves my acting—anyway, because of her, and the sticker on the dashboard, you'll receive preferred parking. You guys head up there and we'll catch up with you in a bit."

"If you're sure you don't want us to help you? Many hands make light work." I loved that saying, even if I didn't entirely know what it meant.

"No, the car is on the next block, right across the road from Starpunds. We'll get these two cleaned up and ready to headline at the solstice."

"There's a Starpunds in Bath?" For a moment I pictured in my head the Roman's making the trek across land, heading to their Aquae Sulis spa for a dip, gold coins in their hands to pay the goddess, but stopping for a sweetened coffee on the way. How much more perfect could life get?

"We are in the twenty-first century," a passerby commented, obviously eavesdropping on our conversation, how rude.

"Here's the keys and drive carefully," Michael advised. "We'll meet you there."

With a backward glance at the four of them, we passed a massive church and crossed at the lights towards Starpunds. Ralb used his brains for once and activated the key fob for us to find the right car.

"This can't be it. It's not even a car. It's more a scooter with four wheels and a roof." The car, and I use the term very loosely, was a bug. No, I mean it was dressed up like it was Halloween. I mean, let's face it, I for one know bugs. This had two antennas sticking out of the roof, bobbing in the slight breeze. It was painted a pea soup shade of green, just one step above vomit-green and when I walked around to the front, the lights, or should I say eyeballs were painted a bright yellow.

"You've got to be kidding me," Jezebel echoed my thoughts. "I can't get into this vee-hicle."

"I totally agree. We have to tell David. Surely, he didn't mean for us to ride in this. He did say it belonged to royalty, maybe the keys got mixed up," I added hopefully.

"Come on you two, it'll be fun. Where's your sense of adventure?"

"Yeah, right. I'll show you an adventure." Just what I need is to get a major backache and or headache before my interplanetary traveling.

I put Pepperpot down, opened her case and let her do her business before the car ride.

"Wow, I've never ridden in a bug before," Jezebel crooned, obviously changing her tune. "I call shotgun."

Shoot! I so should have called it. Dang it all.

"Actually, I left my wallet at home, maybe you should drive," Ralb suggested to her. Good one bro. I'd wondered how he was going to get us to Rockhedge Circle without getting us killed on the A303.

"Sure, no problem." She hopped in on the right side of the car, funny I still can't get used to that after being in the United States.

I had to ask. "Why do you guys drive on the wrong side of the road?"

She adjusted the rear-facing mirror, and then used it to glare towards me. "We drive on the right side, it's those bloody Yanks who drive on the wrong one." Obviously, this was a sore point and I didn't want to get into an argument as old as the colonies.

With a little bit of maneuvering, not to mention cursing to which I will spare you those details, we finally got on our way.

"So, tell me about David's grandfather. I find it fascinating he went to so many different places and saw so many historical sites." The day was starting to break, the sun just creeping up out of the sky illuminated the scenery. Out the window, I saw picturesque villages and picture postcard homes with thatched roofs. Wild growing gardens without any borders filled in the front of the houses, providing a rainbow of red, white, and purple.

"It's kind of ironic you ask about him on the way to Rockhedge Circle. That was his favorite place of all time and the last time anyone saw him."

Well, that was kind of a conversation killer, if ever I heard one.

Chapter 35

"What happened?" I had to get the conversation back onto a merry note. This might be the only time I was going to be able to pick someone's brain about what my Parental Being got up to on Earth.

"He was obsessed with the rocks, the stones as they were." She slowed down before coming to a bridge, allowing a farmer with a horse and wagon stacked with hay to proceed. He tipped his hat as he passed us. "He had a hair-brained idea about the rocks. Popular belief at the time was the stones were a calendar, others believed when they found red markings, it was a sacrificial site like the pyramids in Mexico."

"What did he believe?" I leaned forward between the seats, accidentally thumping Ralb in the shoulder.

"He went and lay amongst the stones and had a feeling it was a graveyard. Each of the stones were in fact headstones. Again, he compared it to the pyramids of Egypt. Whereas they were built for the kings, the Druids and their followers dragged the rocks by barge and ropes. First, they laid out the circular plan with wood, and then they eventually were replaced by the stones.

"I wonder where he got the idea," I mused.

Jezebel must have hearing like a dog because she continued as if I'd spoken to her. "As I said, he laid down amongst the stones. Back in those days, you were allowed to actually climb on them. A fact people took advantage of and actually used spray paint to destroy them." She shuddered and shifted gears. "I fear what would have happened to our beautiful stones if the Heritage Society hadn't stepped in when they did."

"Horrid," I agreed. I'd noticed that in other countries as well. Who really cared if Tom hearted Kat? Show your love for your intended by flowers or jewelry.

"So, one day when he was lying in the circle, he had the premonition there were bodies buried there. The next morning, he came back with a shovel and hoes and carefully dug where he had the strongest sensations."

"And what did he find?"

"He found the archer. A young man who'd been horribly murdered a long time ago. In fact, the archer's body is now housed in a museum where hopefully the young man is finally at rest. He was a mere twenty-three years old, an archer…"

Wow, that was a lot to take in.

"David's grandfather loved archery and I think he felt a certain kinship to the young man."

"Did he find any more bodies?" I had to know. I caught Ralb's eye and shrugged. Could our Parental Being actually be the archer? Could he have time traveled in a before life and ended up at Rockhedge Circle back in the times it was being formed? Was our Parental Being an actual walking encyclopedia? I had a pile of questions to ask when I next saw him, and I wouldn't take no for an answer.

"Maybe, he went back and stayed for six months, at a time. It's doable," Ralb whispered.

"Were there other bodies found?" I repeated the

question. Thanks to Ralb we'd gotten off topic.

"The archer was the one who made the papers, probably because he died under such gruesome circumstances, but there was another one, one David's grandfather kept under his hat so to speak."

"Go on," I asked, swiveling in the back seat as Jezebel took the turn a little fast. Poor Pepperpot didn't know what happened as she flew across the seat away from me.

"The other body was someone more famous. David's grandfather used small digging tools and it took forever for him to get to the body. He didn't want to dig too far down alongside the rocks, didn't want them to fall over any more than they already were. I used to pack lunches to take with him; he'd be gone all day and night, working sometimes twenty hours a day. Finally, he unearthed his find. He called me, all excited. He didn't want to share his news with me over the phone, he was a tad paranoid. He wanted to tell me himself."

"And what did he say? What was his news?" I was literally on the edge of my seat waiting to hear what David's grandfather had discovered.

"Well, I don't know. He never made it home and I never saw him again.

Chapter 36

"Personally, I think he was bumped off." She signaled and turned right, narrowly missing a rock wall. "To me, it was the biggest conspiracy of its day. A man of his age and stature doesn't just disappear."

"So, what do you think happened?" I was interested. She was his confidante, probably knew more about what was going on in his life than anyone else. "Did the gypsies take him?"

"I think aliens abducted him." Feasible, but I wanted to hear her explanation. "I think they were finished making the crop circle and I don't know, maybe he saw their spaceship and decided he knew too much." She kept the car on the straight road, upshifting when she hit a straightaway. "Did you know England sees more UFO's than any other country? And I think you know why."

Probably, I wanted to say but, of course, didn't. People need to believe what they need to and frankly, you know how I feel about alien encounters.

"Because the chalk drawings are their maps. They know if they follow the trotting horses, they'll come to the Giant who will show them the way."

Alrighty then. Yeah, because we can interplanetary travel at the drop of a hat while you Earthlings are still at the rocket ship stage and we need maps to figure out where we're going.

Hello! We invented maps, that's how the early explorers found out where they were going, for the most part, using the stars, and the brightest one—Zorca-twenty-three.

The traffic came to a standstill and in the distance, I could see floodlights flashing in the sky. A police officer or 'Bobby' saw our car and waved us through. How cool was that? I felt like royalty but wondered why every police officer in England was called Bobby? Like when mothers had babies, did they know if they called it Bobby he was guaranteed to have a job as a cop?

Personally, I couldn't wait for the stupid sun to rise, I've had enough of the darkness.

"Park up there," he ordered, waving his flashlight like it was a music conductor's baton. "Then follow the crowds. The show should start in about half an hour."

Before we could answer him, he walked to the car behind us and waved them towards a different area. Poor visitors. I wonder if he was impressed by the Royal sticker on the windshield or the bug outfit our car was dressed in.

A man dressed as a druid passed us, his long white gown decorated with red embroidery. A long white beard flowed almost to the brown cord belt at his waist.

Jezebel walked over to the man and without blinking her eyes, brought her fist back and clocked him right in the chin. He staggered backward and landed against the car. "That's for David."

Without another word, Jezebel locked the door and gave Ralb the keys. "Can you hang on to them? I have a bad habit of losing stuff." She grabbed tightly onto Ralb's arm. "I don't want to lose you."

"Sure." He pocketed them. "Let's get this party started."

I climbed over the seat and got out the passenger side. The man was rubbing his chin and grimacing. "Jezebel, what the heck did I ever do to you?"

"Nothing to me, Even Childs but you made David and Michael's life a living pain."

I got out and stretched. I tried to no avail to work the kinks out of my neck and back. I was going to be in bloody agony tomorrow. Of course, Ralb left me to carry everything. I had Pepperpot tucked in her carry bag and Rotsen in the side pocket of my *hanuglug.* I rushcd to keep up with those two.

Sounds from an ancient flute filled the air as well as the strong aroma of mint.

Inhaling Jezebel smiled. "Oh, it smells like home in the caravan."

"Wait! Stop! I have to use the bathroom." I'd noticed the blue buildings as well as the line-ups. I knew they wouldn't get any shorter and I didn't know if my full bladder would be able to handle space travel.

"Fine, we'll meet you over by the big rock," Ralb waved his hand dismissively. "Don't be long, the sun is ready to rise."

"So, like, Bryan wants me to go all the way with him here and I don't know what to tell him." A teenage girl, her hair stripped yellow and blue chomped gum and unbuttoned her blouse even more.

"Don't do it," her friend suggested, and I silently pumped my fist in the air. "It's not worth it. Do you really want your first time to be with Bryan? He was with Sally last week and Sylvia the week before." The girl took a small mirror out of her pants pocket and squinted her eyes together. "What do you think of this eye shadow? I have to say I'm really not a fan of it, the color sucks."

"Yeah, it doesn't look good on you." Wow, this girl was as mean to her friend as Suzz used to be to me before I stood up to her. "Wow, would you look at that bird?" She pointed to the albino crow on top of the outhouse. "What kind of bird would want to come here?"

Suddenly my bladder felt empty, but it was my stomach that felt nauseous. I bent over and lost my dinner, lunch, and breakfast.

"Oh yuck," the girl in front of me screamed. "She just missed my shoes. Geez, if you can't handle your booze, you shouldn't be drinking."

You guessed it by my reaction.

The bird was Gorget.

It had hunted me down and if I knew my ex-mawlfriend, this wasn't going to be a pretty reunion.

Chapter 37

I could run. I could hide. He wouldn't be able to find me amongst all the people. I glanced down at what I was wearing and grimaced. The clothes I wore weren't perfect, with a bird's keen eyesight, he'd be able to hunt me down.

"Here, you go ahead." The 'nice' girl gestured to me. I nodded a thanks and headed inside. Like a quick-change artist, I removed my clothes, switching them with ones in my *hanaglug,* and slowly exited the outhouse.

The bird obviously figured I'd be in there longer because as in the manner of Gorget, he was on top, preening his feathers. I took the opportunity to head into the crowds, hopefully to disappear.

"What's the rush?" Rotsen asked, no doubt a bit dizzy from my darting walk.

"Gorget has found us. Sorry." I apologized to the young couple kissing on the ground who I almost stepped on.

"Oh stars. Okay, pull me out and I'll be our telescope. We have to find Ralb and get the show on the road."

I headed us towards the rock while Rotsen kept a lookout above and behind us. I caught sight of Ralb and Jezebel, only to lose them. I tripped over a cord, leading to the stage where some stagehand forgot to tape up. I did a face plant into the dirt and skinned my knee, exposed from my skirt.

"Here let me help you up," a familiar voice offered.

"No, I'm good thanks." Cripes, I thought I'd hid from Gorget but he managed to find us.

I turned over and sat up and screamed. I shrieked like the femawl I am. Yelled at the top of my two lungs. You would too if the love of your life suddenly showed up.

"Josh, oh my gosh, is it really you?"

Chapter 38

I leaped to my feet like I had fire ants in my pants. My arms went familiarly around his neck and I covered his face in kisses. Then his mouth found mine. It was better than I remembered. It was like we were the only two at Rockhedge Circle. The air was suddenly silent. My world was spinning. He grasped each side of my face in his two hands; his brown eyes stared into mine before he lowered his lips to my mouth. First it was soft, butterfly kisses, and then it demanded more. His tongue darted inside my mouth and I gasped. I too, could not get enough of him.

When we came up for breath, I leaned forward for one more.

"How did you find me? I thought I'd never see you again." I couldn't, wouldn't let him go as I grasped his hand.

"Kaj led me away when we'd crash-landed in New Zealand. When I went back to you, you guys were gone. So, I began my search. It was quite the adventure. I hopped cruise ships, and private boats working my way up the coast to England."

"I missed you."

"I so missed you too. I wasn't going to give up until I found you. I love you, April, and I want to be wherever you are."

"Really, you mean that?" I stopped to try and catch

my breath. "What led you to England? How did you know I'd be here? What about your mom?"

Sheepishly he admitted, "I followed Suzz's career. I figured you wouldn't be too far from her and I was right. Mom wants me to be with you."

"Josh." I picked up Pepperpot from the ground. "We're getting ready to travel back to Zorca-twenty-three. Do you really mean it you want to go with me? With us?" I pointed down to the dog. "She was a gift to me from David and Michael."

"Who's David and this Michael?" He sounded weary. "I knew it. I'd travel halfway around the world and if I didn't get here soon enough you'd have someone else taking my spot. It never fails." I couldn't believe it when I saw tears well up in his eyes. "I'll leave you alone."

"Stop! Josh, they are a couple, Michael and David. Get it! They're together. TO GETHER! They have zero interest in me in any way other than as a relative, but that's a story for another day. You are the mawl I love. I've always loved you. You are my soul mawl. While others must search cross country, we had to go a little further, but we found each other and I for one am not going to let you go. Look, I'm wearing your ring."

"Geez, why don't you two get a room?" Ralb said, coming up to us. "Oh, I see Josh found you."

"You knew he was here?" I wanted to punch my brother but for once I didn't care. I was too happy.

"Hey, chillax, sister. I saw him when you were waiting for the potty. Speaking of which, that's where I left Jezebel. So, if we're going to ditch her so we can do some space traveling, we'd better get going."

"Ralb, you just can't leave her here stranded. She's

an old lady."

"Don't worry about old Jezebel. She's already found three men she's 'shared some history with,' and David is here somewhere so she'll be good."

We wandered through the crowds, towards the stage, where the biggest rock stood.

"May I have your attention please," a voice called out from the loudspeaker. "One, two, one, two. Quiet please."

Slowly the crowd silenced as if as one they could sense the importance of this announcement. The sun was rising in the sky, the burning orb causing a wave of excitement to rush through the crowds.

I searched overhead for Gorget, the bird, and was relieved to see nothing in the vicinity, other than a news helicopter waiting to film the momentous occasion. A clear sky on the morning of the summer solstice. Life doesn't get any better.

"I'm Rita Wood, live from Channel 3, and are we all having a good time?" A cheer arose from the crowd. "There's good news and bad news. First the good news."

"Despite tremendous odds, Peach Acid is here to play for us, albeit without Freaky Freddie but with American star, Suzzy."

Another deafening cheer rose up.

"As a special treat, we have the helicopter landing in the field and our very own The Bees are going to play for us."

"Wonder why they got The Bees here, surely the attention of the rocks should be enough to keep the folks entertained?" My smart mawlfriend questioned.

"Now the bad news." She waited until the crowd

quieted somewhat. "Due to recent road constructions, the rocks are not in the same position they were when they were built." The announcer read from a card. "Due to the fact, for the previous five years of clouds and rain, we didn't have the summer solstice, we now realize the sun will not be climaxing through the rocks."

A loud boo emanated.

"Oh gosh, I hope the crowds don't get rowdy," Ralb said, preparing to run.

"Well, I guess we're stuck here once again," Rotsen confirmed.

"No way. There must be some way we can get back to Zorca-twenty-three?

"The Church."

Chapter 39

"The Church!" we said as one. Well, Ralb and I, Josh didn't have a bonafide clue what on Earth we were talking about.

"What church?" Josh asked, glancing between Ralb and me, then back to me.

"When I stayed with David and Michael, I lived in their house which was formally a church. The corner stone was actually two stones and they are the same type as the ones at Rockhedge Circle, same radiocarbon dating." We had to get back to the church. The summer solstice might not be hitting the stones at Rockhedge Circle in the right position but we had a plan B.

Our fellow revelers stood in shock; no doubt saddened by the news but then the memory became apparent about the fact they were about to see another English Icon.

Suzz took the stage, surrounded by David and Jocko. They obviously cleaned up well because they now looked like they belonged on the pages of Cheery magazine.

The first familiar strands began of their hit song.

"Come on!" Rotsen shouted at us, to get us into gear. Luckily because of our Royal sticker status at the festival, our car was parked just outside the gate. Ralb unlocked the doors and jumped into the right side. Josh and I in the back as Rotsen wrapped himself around the steering wheel and gave the orders.

Obviously, he'd seen too many movies because he ordered Ralb to reverse the car and we almost hit the vehicle behind us. Thank stars there was now a fence around Rockhedge Circle or with his driving history, he might have run over a few more stones. Severe whiplash spun through my already sore neck and shoulders. Back and forward each of our heads bobbed in unison, as they tried to work the stick shift.

"Want me to drive?" Josh asked, letting go of my hand. "I do have a driver's license."

"Fine, whatev." Ralb shifted over to the left side and after a quick kiss on my cheek, Josh climbed through and settled into the front. Smoothly like we were riding on a sea of smooth chocolate, we headed along the A344, toward Bath.

"Train or car?" Josh asked as he slowed down at the station.

"I vote car," I said, the voice of reason. "We'd have to change trains at Paddingstone Station. Besides, every cop is going to be at the festival."

"True!" Josh stepped on the gas and our bug hit speeds it had never encountered before.

I didn't want to distract Josh, but I couldn't help staring at him. He was even better looking than I remembered. There was contentment, a masculinity about him, which made him even sexier. Not to mention the cute beard that wasn't on his face, more like his chin. It was so straight; you could lay a ruler across it. But the best thing about him in my opinion was he was in love with me, and all my baggage. Which when you're a planet traveling Teenage Alien isn't your average Jerry Winter episode.

"How long do we have to make the summer solstice?" Josh asked taking his eyes from the road to turn around and ask me.

"Geez, would you two get a room!" Rotsen pulled his head around so he was once again facing the road. "I have the *mist book* right here." He popped it open, and then flipped through till he found the right section. "According to this, and I quote. 'At a secondary site, one has until sunset of the morning of the summer solstice to use the rocks as a springboard for interplanetary travel.'"

"It really says springboard?" Josh asked, trying to see the book. Unfortunately, to a mortal, it comes across as a really thick fog.

"Yes, and furthermore," Rotsen said, now perched on the dashboard, his stem wrapped around the radio knob. "There's no need to speed which is just as well because there's a cop coming up behind us."

****

"Well, that was an experience," Josh mumbled. "I hate lying to cops."

"You did very well." I kissed him. Only Ralb's scowl prevented me from taking it further. "He was like putty in your hands and he did tell us about a big accident further down the road."

"Great! Which is going to add even more time onto our trip." Rotsen complained.

"Right! I bet the cow that got hit by the tractor and is tying up the lanes really did it to ruin your day."

I kinked my neck in trying to catch Ralb's eye. "Death? Do you think that was the death Hildy was talking about?"

"Must be. Anyway, can we get this sorry show on

the road?" Ralb asked, settling back into the passenger seat.

"Would you mind switching spots with April?" Josh asked, somewhat a lot nicer than I do when dealing with Ralb

"Yeah, I call shotgun." Not really knowing what the saying means but liking the sound of shotguns around my brother. "Besides, I want to sit beside Josh."

I snuggled in beside him, it was hard not to be close in the small confines of the car and once again we headed towards London. Once he got the car in fourth gear, we were able to hold hands.

Ralb sulked in the back seat, his head permanently pressed against the window.

"So, tell me how you've been keeping yourself amused since I saw you in New Zealand?" I asked.

"I searched for you the next day and was told by Kaj you told her you hated me, never wanted to see me again and in your own words to 'bug off.'"

"What! I never…what a lying sneak." I actually thought of stronger, meaner words but I'm not sure how old you are, and I don't want to ruin your mind with my foul language.

"I couldn't believe it either and I wanted to hear it from you, so I began my search." He smiled. "I felt like I was searching for my family and in a way I was." Aww, how could you not love this mawl? I squeezed his hand and he continued. "I worked on a cruise ship, from New Zealand to Africa, got another one in Africa, and eventually made it to England."

"But how did you know about Rockhedge Circle and the summer solstice?"

"A little voice kept urging me on."

"And yes, it was me." Rotsen bowed. "I never got you a birthday present, and with the *mist book* I could see what he was up to."

"You never told me the *mist book* could track people?" Once again, I was astonished with what this square blanket of fog could do.

"Would you look at that?" Ralb interrupted. He wound the window down and hung his head out. "There's a horse on a hill."

"Yeah, which apparently our Parental Being made."

"I know that," Ralb snarled. "But it's moving."

"It's because you're in a moving car, that's why it seems like it is."

"*No, look!*" I did and I did a double-take, which didn't do my neck any favors. The horse was now standing beside the Giant, and they were both walking across the hills.

"What do you think that means?" Josh asked, momentarily taking his eyes off the road.

"They are our signals, like a gatepost to the summer solstice," Rotsen confirmed. "What? I don't want to give away all my secrets, and then you won't have a need to keep me around."

"Aww, are you kidding me?" I reached up and hugged him and Pepperpot even licked Rotsen's petals. "There's always a place for you in my life."

"In our lives," Josh corrected.

"Get me a barf bag I'm going to be sick," Ralb complained from the back seat.

Chapter 40

Skidding to a stop in front of David's church, we ran up the path and headed inside.

"Now what?" I asked, holding Pepperpot under one arm, linking fingers with Josh, and having Rotsen wrapped around my neck. "Quick we're losing our light. What does the *mist book* say?"

A glow shone through the octagon window, flashing as if lightning was occurring on the other side. Either that or a streetlight on its way to burning out.

"I think it has something to do with the glass in the window." As one we walked towards it and stood staring at the weird markings. "Anybody getting anything?"

A pecking at the window interrupted us. As one we looked at it and saw the white bird pecking a hole through.

"We have to hurry. We can't let Gorget come with us."

The unusual markings lit up, one at a time before fading to black.

"Wait! I think I've got it." Rotsen said, flipping through the *mist book* so fast, the pages were giving me a wonderful facial. "Each of those markings stand for a letter in the Earth Alphabet. S. T. O. N. E. S. A. L. O. N. E"

"What the heck is sto nesa lone?" Ralb asked. "I

don't get it."

"Stones alone," Josh confirmed. "We have to look to the stones."

"He's right." As one we headed towards the two stones where a faint crack of sun was showing. "Look, I saw these marks before with David."

when the sun day
reaches its peak
you shall find
what you so
seek

Rotsen followed his leaf across the marks:
"We chant as one.
When the sun reaches its peak
You will find what you so seek."

We chanted like we were cheering on our football team. We made it once completely through the stanza, and just as the word 'peak' left our combined lips, I felt a suction.

Strong!

I grabbed tighter onto Josh and he hugged me with Pepperpot squished in the middle. The suction grew stronger, stronger, stronger until we meshed into a mist, flung between the cracks, and out into space.

Twirling, twisting, we went as one long stream, a rainbow of colors flashed in front of my eyes. We whipped through a zoo, inside and outside of cages, and we almost got stuck in the bars before a strong pull got us out of there. The lion was shocked at the intrusion of his space. Acid and a stomach upsetting smell of sewage passed my nose. Geez, no matter what shape Ralb took, he had to pass wind. Ironically Ralb's shoe hit me in the stomach as we spiraled up into the atmosphere.

I didn't know where we'd end up but wherever it was, I would be home. Because home is where your heart is, and it belonged to Josh totally, well, maybe a little piece was taken by Pepperpot.

A word about the author…

Born with a passion to read and write and heavily influenced by Nancy Drew mysteries, Jane Greenhill recalls her first writing experiences on an old Underwood typewriter, plunking away at the keys while she wrote about hiding clues in oak trees. Fast forward through marriage and motherhood and Jane's now advanced to a laptop and her characters speak to her from other planets.